SOULLESS

JADE WEST

CHAPTER ONE

Elaine

I USED TO dream about it late at night—being kidnapped by a monster.

There was a strange dread and fascination with being taken. Owned. It was no different in real life, walking away from my apartment complex at the side of Lucian Morelli.

He didn't speak to me, because no words were needed. I knew he was my god from here on in. I was nothing more than a little doll in his sadist show.

That's what he was. A sadist. A sadist who wanted my blood.

I had no doubt he'd be taking it, slowly and painfully.

I was the one who broke the silence. "Where are we going?"

He could have told me it was none of my

business, and I would've still followed him. I had no choice. Not while my best friend in the world was being held for ransom if I didn't obey. Tristan's life was worth more to me than mine.

"We're going to get a cab," the monster said, just like that.

We could have called a car on his phone easily enough, but I guess he didn't want to. The anonymity of a taxi must have been a more appealing option. It made sense.

A Morelli with a Constantine in any form would be remarkable in our world.

Lucian's eyes were fixed ahead of us, glittering in their darkness. His jaw looked as firm as ever from my angle, looking up at the beast. It occurred to me for just that second, trotting alongside him on the sidewalk, that he was as unsure of how things were panning out as I was.

It seemed odd that he was acting on impulse, totally out of character with the way he usually reeked of control and structure.

Yeah, he was out of his comfort zone. The thought made me smile a little, even in my fear.

It happened to be the moment he chose to fix me in his stare. "What's funny, sweetheart?" he asks with a taunt in his voice. "Share with the class."

It didn't stop me from smiling. Even now, with the mind-spinning promise of fate ripping me out of this world, there was a beautiful sense of relief in my soul. "Why shouldn't I smile?" I countered. "Maybe I'll be happy when you hurt me. I was about to end my own life, after all."

I thought back to the bottles of pills I'd left behind and how he'd disturbed me from them by turning up at my apartment door. He still had the *Tristan* suicide note I'd written in his inside pocket. It was typical that he'd used it to work out just how important Tristan is to me.

"You've had plenty of chances to end your life. You didn't. Even tonight you were waiting for the big bad wolf to come and take you. You're lying to yourself."

That offended me.

I stopped walking and folded my arms across my chest.

"I wanted to be the one to take my own life," I told him. "It's my life. That was my right."

My heart leapt a little as he turned to face me and stepped close. He loomed tall. His voice was barely more than a hiss when he spoke. "It's not your right anymore, Miss Constantine. You can wave that freedom goodbye. Your life belongs to me now."

I belonged to Lucian Morelli. "Ha!" I couldn't help laughing in his face.

He didn't even flinch. He held out a hand, and I looked down at his outstretched fingers, so big and firm. *He* was so big and firm. It felt weird to take his hand in mine. The power in his grip was…intense…

My heart leapt again as he pulled me along with him.

In that moment, hand in hand on the sidewalk, we must have looked like any regular couple enjoying their evening. If only we were. If only we'd been two people meeting each other at a party and wanting to fuck. If only we'd been two people drawn together without our family war gripping us tight. It was a bizarre truth how instinctively I hated the man holding my hand, and I had since I was old enough to understand his name.

Constantines versus Morellis. Enemies over generations. Malice to the death.

I'd long forgotten even half of what was so terrible that their family had done to ours. More than our family had done to theirs though, that was for sure. That was a mantra I'd learned since I was a toddler. *The Morellis are bad people.*

"You'd better behave in the cab," the monster

told me as the stand came into view. "Even so much as a squeak for help will lead to nothing but the death of your friend."

Part of me doesn't want to believe him. It's one thing to defend your family and your territory. Another thing to hurt an innocent like Tristan. I think Lucian is just bluffing...but he might not be. "Don't insult my intelligence by thinking you have to tell me that. I'm well aware what an evil piece of shit you are, Lucian Morelli."

His mouth pressed up to my ear. "I'm well aware of what a little liar you are too, Elaine Constantine. And I'm going to make you suffer for it."

I shivered as we stepped up to the first cab in the line. Lucian held the door open for me. What a gentleman. I shuffled climbed into the back seat as he joined me. I stared out of the window on the other side, looking anywhere but at the man setting out to destroy me.

You wanted him to take you, murmured a low, raspy voice in my head. *You've always been a slut. You've always wanted men to hurt you.*

I shivered in the cool leather seat. There was a strange bond between us. Attraction. Lust. Or maybe something far more base—an exchange of power.

We were like two poles of a magnet, drawn together.

And I couldn't deny that I would have fought harder, would have used my teeth and nails to escape another man bent on kidnapping me. With Lucian Morelli, I was willingly going along.

He leaned forward to the driver, keeping himself as low-key as possible, no doubt, as he cleared his throat and pasted on a sad little smile.

"Bishop's Landing," he said, and my stomach lurched.

The seat of my family's power. And the seat of his. The Morellis and the Constantines had both occupied the affluent town for generations. Why two warring families would choose to live so close together, I would never understand. There was even a joke sometimes, whispered among those feeling particularly brave, that the massive feud had once started over a neighborly dispute. They would take something regular neighbors fight about and make it something extravagant. *They must have been fighting over their diamond encrusted fence.* Or, *their exotic tiger probably ate the miniature chihuahua who lived alone in the pool house next door.*

It was the place my kidnapper was driving me

to, a place where he would be at risk for discovery, a place where he had allies all around him.

It was a place of contradiction. Of risk.

Of an almost self-destructive form of courage.

Farewell, New York City.

Hello, hometown.

CHAPTER TWO

Lucian

ELAINE CONSTANTINE WAS a little blonde butterfly driving me insane in that back seat. Her pursed lips were still holding onto her spite, trying to be a little firebrand in my grip. It only made me even more desperate to toy with her.

I knew I was playing with fire, taking things to the next level when I told the cab driver Bishop's Landing. It was almost an hour from New York City. I could've caged Elaine in my Manhattan apartment for a few long days safely enough without any questioning, and that's what I should have been going for—a few long days with the butterfly before I ripped her wings off one by one. But I didn't. My filthy heart wouldn't let me give up my dirty little plaything so soon. I wanted every damn fucking second with her I could claim.

Bishop's Landing was the answer.

It was the heart of both the Constantines and the Morellis. A fitting place for me to consummate my obsession. Despite the fact that it was our family seat, I rarely spent time here. My time was usually torn heavily between Morelli Holdings and Violent Delights. Now I drove us to the elaborate estate I owned, far enough away that we could have our privacy. No one would hear her when she screams my name.

She was watching the mansions rolling past outside, trying her best to feign disinterest.

Her blonde hair was alive under the glow of the passing streetlights. Her slim delicacy made her look like a porcelain puppet ready to be worked by the puppet master. I was glad that I was proving to be the puppet master, not the fucking Power brothers.

I approached them and confirmed her debt. Over three hundred and fifty thousand dollars. Not her own money spent on drugs or gambling. She was paying off the debt of men and women who had children. She was, in her own twisted, party girl way, trying to make the world a better place.

"I know you're looking at me, Lucian," she said. "I can feel the lust in your eyes."

She wasn't wrong.

I didn't reply.

Even afraid, she wanted me.

We were opposites, drawn together inexorably. Both of us, transfixed by the black magic of our flesh. Not to mention she had an incredible body.

I could still feel her tight ass milking my cock dry from where I'd claimed her. Still feel the mix of rage and desire in her. Rage because she thought she was going to get a good fucking for the first time in her sorry life. Desire because she loved it. Loved *me* fucking her dirty little asshole. I'd been reliving the thrill over and over.

The memory was burned into me—fucking her Constantine ass in a pool of another man's blood. I'd butchered him for touching her. I knew it would be burnt into her, too.

We were both snared with our own mutual hate and filth intertwined.

We were both well into the depths of the forbidden from both fucking families. I'd crossed the line the very first moment I'd kissed her at Tinsley Constantine's ball.

May as well get my twisted thrill from her.

The streets turned into stretches of open road surprisingly quick. The silence grew heavy as we grew closer to our destination. The cab driver said nothing, just kept his eyes ahead.

I only hoped we were doing a decent enough job at feigning a regular life in a regular world. "Up here on the left," I told him, and directed him up the driveway to my place.

My Bishop's Landing house was one of the smallest in the town. It was also one of the most expensive. Every piece of marble was hand selected from India. The cloths used to wrap each large plate cost more than most people made in a year.

Yes, the Morelli family had money.

Old money. New money. We had all the fucking money we needed.

The fight over the company was never really about money. My father and I both had enough to play with private jets as if they were toy cars. This was about power. The power to support the family and control its pursestrings. The power to help my siblings the way I never did as a child. The fates of tens of thousands of employees, whose livelihoods hung in the balance.

And I'd failed. Given up. Were those the right words?

Perhaps it would be more correct to say I'd traded that in for Elaine Constantine. The woman

I shouldn't want. The woman my body couldn't live without.

Of course, the smallest house in Bishop's Landing was still 8,000 square feet. And I had over an acre of land. We pulled down the white-gravel road and rolled to a stop at the front of the door. *A contemporary monstrosity,* my mother had said when she saw the architect's designs. *In Bishop's Landing? Darling, think of its illustrious history.* It wasn't contemporary actually. It was mid-century modern, but my mother didn't understand style that didn't include gilt scrolls. She thought mid-century modern was one of those California hippie things. Like feng shui. Or pot.

"Here," I said, and the cab pulled up at the top of the driveway. The place was pitch dark. Massive glass panes rose above us, looming in a perfect, jagged edge. Imported white quartz bricks gleamed faintly in the moonlight. A few military-straight bushes lined the front.

It gave me a little shiver of lust to see Elaine trying so hard to see our destination in the shadows. Here we were, at the cage of her torment. I was the big bad wolf waiting to tear open his prey. It was a civilized lair, but there was nothing civilized about the way I wanted her.

"Keep the change," I told the driver and handed over just a sliver more than the right amount. Nothing too obvious or notable. Nothing for him to remember if he's questioned.

Elaine didn't have a last-minute freak-out as I opened her door for her. She didn't have a burst of *save me!* for the driver. She didn't try to run off into the night.

No. She was a good girl. She stepped out of the cab and resigned herself to her fate like a sweet little lamb to the slaughter.

I watched the cab rumble away down the driveway before I dug the keys out of my pocket. I'd barely used them over the past year, too caught up in Morelli Holdings and business life to scrape even a scrap of time away from the city.

I left Elaine standing on the spot as I headed up to the front door. Even with my back to her, I knew she was staring intently over at me with her heart in her throat as I pushed the key into the lock and opened the door, ready and waiting.

"Come on in and meet your fate," I said and led the way inside.

CHAPTER THREE

Elaine

I T WASN'T WHAT I was expecting from him. Not in the slightest.

The house was small and strangely cozy, despite the metals and woods and glass used in the design. It somehow worked together in harmony, making me feel at ease.

It wasn't exactly the billion dollar bachelor pad I would've pictured for the Morelli heir.

He must've seen the surprise in my eyes as I crossed the threshold and stepped into the hall. My gaze was flitting around the place, checking out the decor. Artwork on the wall. Paintings? No, they were made out of wood and other materials. They were a cross between a picture and a sculpture, with geometric designs and stark contrasts. A rich cherry wood traced through a matte black canvas, with streaks of burnished gold.

"What does it mean?" I asked, forgetting for one moment that he was my enemy.

"It's pain," he said. "At least the way I imagine it would feel."

I gave him a disbelieving look. "You don't know what pain feels like? Is that some sort of weird rich boy flex, like nothing has ever hurt you in your two-thousand thread count sheets?"

"Not quite," he murmured, though he didn't sound offended. More like amused.

"Whatever, Lucian."

All this talk about imagined pain. He probably just wanted to fuck with me. It didn't matter, anyway. He had money and power and fame. He had a disturbingly handsome face. A lean body.

And the absolute surety that the world was made to please him.

He stepped through to the kitchen, and again it had beautiful smooth spaces. The coffee machine looked like the most expensive item in the building. It had so many silver pipes and steam holes that it reminded me of a luxe Dr. Seuss instrument.

"Are you going to fuck me tonight, then?" I asked him, pasting on my bravest face.

"I'll fuck you whenever it suits me," he told

me, and he meant it.

I looked at him fresh in these new surround-ings, as though I was seeing him for the very first time. His darkness was radiating. His strength was brilliant—muscular and sculpted with biological precision. It was a strange thing, just how opposite our family lines were, in every sense of the word.

His hands were like magicians whenever they moved, his fingers beautiful in their dances. His hair was perfect in his styling. I guess it was the intensity of the surroundings, but Lucian Morelli looked even more of a god in this place. His opulence and class was obvious against the planed backdrop.

I leaned against the counter and watched him.

"You're going to really make me suffer, aren't you?" I asked.

"Yes, sweetheart," he said with an evil smile. "I'm going to make you suffer. I'm going to enjoy every second of it. Morelli versus Constantine in the most intimate of ways."

Somehow, even through the dread and the fear churning inside me, intimacy with Lucian Morelli gave me a shudder of something different.

I expected him to fire up the coffee machine, but he didn't. He crossed the room to the refrigerator and pulled out two mineral waters, pouring them into glasses from the shelf.

"Drink," he ordered, and handed one over.

I did what he told me, because I was thirsty, not because I was his meek little servant. Not yet, anyway. He watched me while he sipped at his.

It was another clear light and dark between us both. Another polarity in our souls. He drank mineral water while I drank champagne. I'd never seen him overindulge, let alone have a dependency on it.

Control. He was all about control.

I was all about losing control.

"I hope your ass is still hurting," he said. "I've got plenty of pain to add to it."

I laughed. "It's had worse. I'm not quite so virginal as you think I am. My life hasn't been all that sheltered, asshole."

"You'll tell me all about who's been ass-fucking you, Elaine. Soon enough, I'll know every one of your dirty little secrets."

He was wrong.

I wouldn't tell him anything I didn't want to. He could tear me apart, and I'd still keep my mouth closed tight.

He tipped my face up to his. "I know there are plenty of dirty little secrets behind those pretty blue eyes."

He wasn't wrong on that front. I had enough dirty little secrets to fill a bookshelf.

His fingers slid down my throat, squeezing just a little before slipping my coat from my shoulders and letting it drop to the floor. I didn't fight him.

"Such a pretty little Constantine," he whispered.

I felt like a pretty little Constantine. It was a beautiful darkness, to be wanted by such a demon.

My words were out of my throat before I even realized they were coming, nothing but a breath from my lips.

"Hurt me, monster. Show me what you really are."

I couldn't hold back a gasp as he raised his hand to my face. I was expecting pain, but I didn't get it. No. I got anything but pain. With a slip of his fingers as he gripped my face, Lucian Morelli pushed his thumb inside my mouth.

It was the strangest thing to have the monster's thumb so intimately between my lips, probing so gently. I'd been touched and groped and abused in the most intense of ways through my life, but nothing had ever made me feel as vulnerable as the way he invaded me. His thumb was strong as it explored my mouth, commanding me in the most intimate way. I tried to pull back from him but he pinned me to the counter, making me moan as he petted my tongue.

"Suck," he said, but I didn't suck.

I moved my tongue in nothing more than a flicker, tasting him. I wanted to taste him. I wanted to taste the monster's thumb.

"Suck," he said again, but I still didn't.

He swapped his thumb for two thick fingers, and I tasted him, fresh. Flickering, flickering, flickering with my tongue.

He liked it. I could see it in his eyes. The monster liked it.

"Dirty girl," he growled, and I loved the dark tone in his voice. "Show me that hungry little tongue, I want to see it."

I opened my mouth nice and wide and showed the beast my tongue, still brushing against his fingers as he pulled them free.

I wasn't prepared for him to lower his head so quickly. I wasn't prepared for the way he nipped his teeth around my tongue hard enough to make me squeal. I tried to pull away, but he grabbed my hair in his fist, held me still as he sucked on my tongue.

I tasted blood at the same time he did.

He let out a moan. I knew he was smiling.

Lucian Morelli really was a monster.

His lips were red as he pulled away.

"You're fucked up," I told him. "Did you know that, Morelli? You're a fuck-up."

I thought he'd take offense, but he didn't. He smirked at me.

"Yes, I know that," he told me. "I've been a fuck-up since the day I was born. I enjoy it. Regular life is so fucking dull."

That made me smirk right back at him. It was one of the few things we had in common. I too had been a fuck-up since the day I was born.

Everyone else in my family had been in their billionaire childhood dreams, and I'd been drifting along the sidelines, focused on the shadows at the edges. Maybe that's why the evil men had picked me out of the Constantine girls for their sick thrills. Maybe I was asking for it with my weird little ways right from the start.

My bleeding tongue was throbbing. I rubbed my mouth on the back of my hand and there was a smear of red. Still, I didn't care. I really was crazy with all my parts jarred together.

I would've happily stayed there for a sick, twisted lifetime, pinned by the filthy fuck-up at the countertop, but no. He had other plans.

His grip was firm on the back of my hair as he spun me around and shoved me back through to the hallway.

"Let the games begin," he said.

Chapter Four

Lucian

HER BLOOD WAS still beautifully metallic in my mouth as I shunted her through to the hallway and onwards, right through to the small library on the property. I almost regretted bringing her here, because it felt as though her eyes were peering inside me somehow.

I switched on a lamp, illuminating her just enough to give her a sweet golden sheen.

"Strip," I told her, and she spun to face me, fixing me in that pretty gaze of hers.

This time she didn't attempt to argue with me. She slipped her dress straps from her shoulders with her lips tight, trying to hold the *fuck you* in her stare. She failed to hide the truth of it, even though her whole body was lying. She was scared.

Really fucking scared.

My mouth watered at the thought of her stomach fluttering, nervous.

I wanted to feel her breaths quick and hot against me as I played with her, but I held back, stoic and firm as I folded my arms across my chest.

"Strip for me," I told her again.

She let the dress slip down to show her bra, perfect in its lacy white sweetness. Her hips held barely any resistance, letting the fabric slide right down her legs to the floor.

White panties. Sweet little white panties.

Jesus Christ, I was going to enjoy her body.

She was already reaching around for her bra clip when I clipped out a *no* to her.

She paused, eyes wide.

"Not yet," I growled. "Stand still like a good girl."

She stood still, but her expression wasn't anything like a good girl. There was a mist of rebellion about her, along with her fear. Fear and want. She wanted me, but hated it.

Just like I wanted her. How I hated that I wanted her.

She was a Constantine.

Not even a useful one. I couldn't use her to regain my company. I couldn't even have her while I completed the coup that had been years in the making. No, I'd had to make a choice. I resented her for making me choose her. For being so beautiful, so broken, so strong that I had to take her for myself. I resented her, even though it hadn't been her choice.

I made her stand for long slow minutes, loving how she shuffled more and more as I stared at her. She was getting agitated along with nervous, until she finally wrapped her arms around herself and found her voice. "Well, are you going to do something to me then or what?"

"Not yet, little doll. I'm going to savor every second."

She sighed at me, feigning a whole new flash of confidence. "Boring, then. Great. May as well have popped the pills and fucked off out of life before you showed up."

I had a sick adoration of these different sides to the butterfly, so many colors on her wings flashing bright. Her fears, her secrets, her need to be a good little girl. Her self-hate, her self-harm, her sad little desire to move on from her upbringing and its bullshit—saving those addicts from the Power brothers. Her mother wouldn't piss on any of them if they were burning, much less allow her daughter to vouch for their debts.

Elaine knew that, too. She knew it and went against her family's will.

I was fascinated by her. "Spread your legs," I told her, and my voice was laced with malice.

"No."

"Spread your legs," I told her again, but she shook her head.

"Make me. I'm not just a little doll who's going to dance to your beat."

I closed the distance between us, loving how she flinched as I stepped up to her. "Oh, you're a little doll, Elaine. You're going to dance nice and hard to my beat."

My cock was straining in my pants, and my mouth was watering. Her breaths were every bit as shallow and fast as I imagined. I could almost hear her heartbeat thumping.

My words were growls, and the dynamic shifted between us.

"Spread your fucking legs."

She shuddered, wanting. She couldn't help but want me.

"Do it," I muttered.

She liked that. Fuck, she liked that. I could feel it.

My cock liked it too. My cock liked it when Elaine Constantine shifted her legs apart.

I crept my fingers up her thigh nice and slowly, tickling. She flinched as my thumb brushed her slit through her wet panties, breaths growing more shallow as I teased.

"I'm going to hurt your pussy," I told her. "I'm going to hurt your pussy so fucking bad you're going to cry for me."

"At least fuck me first."

"You'll have to earn that," I said. "Earn my cock like a good little doll."

There was something about my words that were resonating. I could feel her tension.

"Rub your slit on my fingers," I told her. "Make yourself come."

I teased her, coaxed her, tickling her pussy enough to make her tense up.

I don't know how we did it, descended into such a natural dance of flesh. The dam broke in my dirty girl as she braced herself on me, arms wrapping around my shoulders as she let her hips do the work.

She rubbed her slit on my fingers, fast. She was desperate, walls breaking as her butterfly colors shimmied.

I wouldn't help her. My fingers were strong and still against her as she worked for her thrill.

"Put them inside me," she whispered. "Please."

But no. I wouldn't put them inside her. "Rub your slit," I said. "Come for me."

"Help me," she said, whimpering, rubbing fiercely. "Help me come."

But no. I wouldn't help her come. I wanted the little doll to do it all on her own. "What do you think about when you touch your clit at night?" I asked her with a growl. "What makes you wet?"

The question made her rub harder, putting more weight against my fingers.

"Tell me," I snarled. "What makes you wet, Elaine?"

"Help me," she whispered. "Help me come...please..."

"What makes you wet, Elaine?"

Her rhythm became faster, harder. "Please, Lucian...help me..."

"What makes you touch your clit at night?"

She was shivering, desperate. Her arms were gripping me tight. "Please, Lucian..."

I knew she'd done it before. I knew she'd come for people. "Did they make you touch yourself?" I asked her. "Did they make you touch yourself as they hurt you?"

She tensed, even as she rubbed against me.

Yes. They made her touch herself as they hurt her. I knew it. I knew they hurt her, and I knew they made her like it.

The thought made me hard and full of hate, both at once.

Who the fuck had hurt Elaine Constantine?

"They did it, didn't they?" I whispered. "They made you want it?"

It tipped her over the edge. Her shudder was intense, her bucks so frantic as she cried out. The doll's back arched as she broke herself and came for me. She was lost, her body giving up the fight. Elaine Constantine came against my fingers.

And then I lost her. She came to her senses with a frown, pulling herself away from me with eyes full of spite. She grabbed her scrap of a dress up from the floor and held it tight.

"Fuck you, Lucian! I didn't want it! They could never make me want it. They were repulsive pieces of shit. I hated everything they did to me. And I hate everything you're doing to me."

"If only your clit believed you."

That's when I saw the crack into her soul, right into the depths of her broken heart.

It was absolutely fucking beautiful.

"Do me a favor and get it over with already. Fuck me. Hurt me. Bash my head open, I don't care!"

I make a *tut-tut* sound. "And ruin something so beautiful? I don't think so."

CHAPTER FIVE

Elaine

I HATED THE monster in front of me, playing me so hard for his sick thrills. I should never have let my guard down enough to show him even a snippet of my soul.

The beasts had been playing with me for years since I was a girl, holding tight to my innocence while they twisted and twisted. My family wanted my purity. They barely let me grow up, keeping me in a casket of little girl ways, even when my body was changing. Hell, the men exploited that and used it for what they wanted.

I was seventeen years old when the beasts finally changed their games and used me and my flesh in a whole new way, teasing me in a way I didn't understand.

"I mean it," I told Lucian. "I'm done with your bullshit. I'm done with everyone's bullshit."

I hated so much in life, both big and small. I hated the very fact I was holed up here with a Morelli who hated me. I hated how small and weak I felt in my own pit of fears. I hated the undeniable tingles running from my clit through my body.

Fuck knows what the hell was truly going on here, but I was done with it.

I sat myself down on the floor and pulled my knees to my chest. I wouldn't cry for him. No way would I cry for him. I choked back the tears and thought about all the assholes in the world who'd wanted to see me cry. Fuck them. Fuck him. Fuck Lucian Morelli.

"You're a pretty little thing," he told me. "You really are."

I didn't reply. I didn't have anything to say.

"Look at me," he said, but I didn't.

I looked anywhere but at him. I looked at the hand-scraped wooden floor underneath us and at the smooth leather couch in the room. I looked at the gorgeous art above the fireplace.

"I told you to look at me."

I gave him the middle finger, fuck the consequences.

The consequences were instant. He dragged me to my feet and threw me onto the couch, pinning me down with his hand at my throat hard enough to choke me. "Watch it, sweetheart. Rudeness will make your pain all the slower. All the sweeter."

Even now, the scent and the heat of him drove me wild. I was lost to everything, so twisted up and confused by the whole sorry mess of my existence that I didn't have a clue who I was or what I wanted anymore.

Even as I gasped for breath, I couldn't stop myself rocking against him, legs wrapping around his waist. My body knew what I wanted. My body wanted a cock inside me.

My body wanted *Lucian Morelli's* cock inside me.

He could do it...please...he could fucking do it...

I tried to tempt him. My hips were a whole fresh rhythm of grinding and my panties were still wet from me coming against his fingers. It was louder than words.

"You're a pretty little doll," he told me. "Such a temptress. It would be so easy to fuck your virgin hole right now. You're already wet for me. I can feel it. Smell it"

I coaxed him some more, bucking, writhing.

"Did you tempt them like this?" he asked.

"Did they make you want it this much?"

He let go of my throat enough that I could speak. "No. They fucking didn't."

"I'm going to make you tell me all about it," he said, and a distant little part of me wanted him to. That desperate little girl in me wanted to finally speak the truth and have it believed.

But no. No. "You won't make me tell you. I'll be taking my secrets to my grave, not giving them to a Morelli piece of shit."

"Who did this to you, Elaine?" he asked, and even the question gave me a sick pang in my stomach. "Who were the dirty men who broke you?"

"You wouldn't believe me if I told you," I said. "Fuck you, Lucian."

I could feel his cock, hard against me. It would have been so easy to fuck my tight little virgin hole, he was right.

Just a shame Lucian Morelli doesn't take the easy road.

"This is going to hurt," he told me, and pulled away enough to raise his hand.

My legs were still spread open wide when his palm landed hard on my pussy.

It hurt. It hurt enough that I clenched my thighs as tight as they would go and rolled over onto my side, but I was smiling. Somehow, I was smiling. Laughing.

"You're fucked up," he said, stating the obvious. "Seriously, you've got problems."

I caught my breath enough to speak, pussy still hurting. "Yeah, well that makes two of us then, doesn't it? Because I like being hurt. And you like hurting me."

I had no real idea about the monster above me or who the hell or what the hell he really was. I had no real idea who I was, not with all my shattered pieces jarred together, and I didn't want to know.

I didn't want to know anything.

That's when he pressed himself back down onto me, his breaths hot on my face. "I loved pulling the wings from butterflies when I was a boy," he said. "I'll enjoy pulling yours from you."

"I'm not a butterfly," I told him. "I'm a caterpillar in a cocoon who's never been free, rotting from the inside."

"*I'm* rotten from the inside," he whispered, then licked his tongue flat and wet up my cheek.

I felt him shuffling, and I knew what was coming. He was going to do it, positioning himself between my legs just right. Holy shit, my clit was still hurting from his slap.

His fingers squirmed against my panties, tugging them to the side. I heard him unbuckle his pants, shuffling some more to pull them down.

Lucian Morelli's hips were bare against mine. His cock was hot and hard. He was going to do it...Lucian Morelli was going to take my virginity...

"Yes..." I managed to gasp. "Do it...be the man who truly makes me his..."

"You're mine, Elaine Constantine," he snarled. "Believe me, I'll be the man who truly makes you his. I own every dirty little scrap of your soul."

I braced myself. I held my breath. My body was ready. Ready. Ready.

Yes...

But no.

Just like that, the moment was shattered by the blaring ring of his phone from the other room.

He paused, bracing himself, staring down at me like I was a piece of meat he was ready to butcher.

It was clearly someone important to be calling Lucian Morelli at midnight on his personal phone.

It seems he came to the same conclusion.

"Stay still for me," he said and raised himself back up.

He pulled up his pants and headed away. My breaths were ragged as I watched him leave.

Predictably, I didn't stay still. I got to my feet and inched closer to the doorway, stepping up to the hall. I could hear him pacing around in the other room, barking out one side of a conversation.

"What the fuck? Now? It can wait until morning. I mean it, Alto. It can wait until morning…"

The front door stood tall before me. I guess it was basic human instinct that wanted me to make a dash for it. I nearly did it. I nearly opened that door and ran.

I heard Lucian curse as he stomped his way back down the hall. He looked frustrated, raging at something that wasn't a Constantine. Wow. It was a bizarre phenomenon.

"I need to go," he told me.

My breath caught as the potential reality truly dawned. I was spared. For a while, at least.

He led the way upstairs without so much as a look behind him. I was still hovering at the bottom of the staircase when he shot me an aggravated stare.

"One of the most basic fundamentals of being a servant is following the fucking master," he barked, and for once his rage was spitting in a way that wasn't at me.

"I'm not your servant."

"Oh, that's right. You're my little doll. I take you out to play with you. And then I put you away when I'm done. Now go inside your little box."

I didn't bother arguing with him, not this time, just followed him upstairs meekly with barely more than a scowl.

There was no point in arguing.

He was holding the door open at the far end of the landing. Inside was a room with a bed and a bedside table and very little else.

I already knew the door had a lock on it when I stepped over the threshold. I already knew this was going to be my prison until he showed up again as he set me in his evil stare one more time.

"Enjoy your box," he told me, then left me in the dark.

I heard the key in the lock.

Being alone in this room scared me just as much as he did.

Once his footsteps had left me behind, I finally let myself cry.

Chapter Six

Lucian

I LOVED DRIVING, but it rarely happened anymore. I was always too busy, with drivers waiting on my command. It was a surreal thing to start my car from the garage and head back into New York City. The world was usually a blur of city life to me outside the windows, removed from my engagement, but not tonight. Tonight I was amongst it, senses tuned in to the thrill.

Alto was waiting for me at my penthouse. I pulled into the underground parking lot and headed right on up to level thirty-two, giving my nod to security on level thirty-one via the security cameras in the elevator.

Alto raised his eyebrows as I met him at the doorway.

I opened the door and stepped in, not looking back as I stepped on through to the lounge and the glow of the city lights through the windows. "What the fuck is so important that you want to see me at half one in the morning?"

"News. I didn't want to tell you on your phone, but there's been some pretty crazy shit going down. About Elaine Constantine."

I turned to face him, keeping my expression deadpan. "News?"

I waited for the tornado of accusations and questions, but they didn't come.

"Yeah. The Power brothers. Looks like they've taken her. Shit's going down."

"The Power brothers?"

"Fucked up, huh? I mean, people were saying they were gonna make her pay, but nobody really believed it, you know? Apparently, her mother's making threats. There's going to be a war if we're not careful."

Oh the thrill. I could feel it in my veins, my filthy love of the battle about to go down between our families. Surely the Power brothers couldn't be sitting back and taking that kind of accusation. I looked back out at the city lights. "How do they know it was the Power brothers?"

"Don't know," he said. "I've got feelers out for the details."

"You seriously dragged me back here after

midnight just to tell me that the Power brothers have grabbed Elaine Constantine from her apartment? It could have waited until morning."

"Thought it was pretty major news. You've been hunting her down like some kind of stalker. Thought you'd want in on the action as it happened." His mind worked as he stared up at me.

"If that's all, you can fuck off," I told him and gestured him away.

"Your dad already spoke to me," he told me without moving. "He's very interested to know what's going on with Elaine Constantine. More interested than you are, it seems."

The thought flared in me. Of course he would have been interested—trying to rule me out of the Constantine bullshit no doubt. "What did you tell him?"

"Same as I told you. Not a lot, just that the Power brothers have taken her." His mind was still ticking. I could almost fucking hear it.

"Good for you," I said. "I'm sure he's grateful for your double-crossing." My sarcasm was laced with spite. Spite Trenton Alto was well used to, having been my fixer for twelve years.

"Double-crossing?" he asked. "Nah. It's public knowledge on the street that she's been taken. I didn't tell him anything secret. Not who might have really kidnapped her."

"And who would that be?"

He tipped his head, thinking, thinking. "How did you know they took her from her apartment?"

"What?"

"You said the Power brothers grabbed Elaine Constantine from her apartment. They could have taken her from anywhere. How did you know where they took her from?"

I kept my eyes cool and calm. "A lucky guess."

He didn't believe me. He knew me too well for that. Once again I realized I should have killed the fucker a long time ago. His knowledge was my weakness. "She's rarely there," he said. "One hell of a lucky guess, ain't it?"

"If you have something to say to me, then say it."

I stared at my fixer, so much shorter than me with his tough little scowl. I could kill him and be done with it, but I didn't. It seems that every single one of us has our idiocies. Mine was a selfish desire to keep Alto alive to serve me.

He gestured to my suit. "Lucian Morelli, out for the night, knows Elaine Constantine has been snatched from her apartment…some people might ask questions."

"Not people who had any sense in them."

He held up his hands. "Sure thing, Lucian. Sure thing. Just saying. People will be asking a lot of questions about Elaine Constantine and what the fuck happened to her."

"You'd better keep me informed of them. Me before my father. He can wait in line for the news."

"You before Bryant. I'll be back with news as soon as I get it." He saw himself out without even an attempt at a goodbye. No point making niceties with a bastard like me.

He'd learnt that well enough over the last decade.

It was unlike me to feel any sense of relief or nervousness. It was unlike me to feel *anything* in my psychopathic mind. Feelings were a novelty. Still, I felt them both in that moment. A clash that had my insides tense.

I should've learnt from my own bullshit and the chaos about to kick off in the world around me. I should've taken over Morelli Holdings and left her to die. But I didn't.

Fuck that temptress and her filthy fucking ways, but I didn't.

I barely gave Alto any time to leave the complex before I was straight back down to the parking lot and slipping back into my car. Elaine Constantine was going to get me at my best.

CHAPTER SEVEN

Elaine

THE DARKNESS HAD me wrapped up tight. The light wasn't working overhead. There was a bed in the room, but I didn't want to use it. I was pressed up against the wall opposite the door with my arms around my knees, hugging myself tight.

So many nights I'd been scared in the darkness staring at a locked door. Waiting. Waiting for people. *Men.*

Now I was waiting for one man. Was he really a man? Or was he a monster?

It was hard to tell them apart sometimes.

I was thirsty and cold. Alone.

I was the broken girl I'd been running away from for years, only now I had no cocaine or alcohol to help me escape her. Fuck, I needed it. I needed the escape.

The irony was that no one would think to look for me, not in Lucian Morelli's home. They would check my apartment. Then ask Tristan. He would worry about me. No one would connect me with Lucian Morelli, and even if they did, no one had enough power to compel a search warrant for his home. It was both an obvious and a perfect place to stash a captive. Like hiding the incriminating letters in plain sight.

I really was at Lucian Morelli's mercy now. He could leave me here to shrivel and die and nobody would ever know it. As much as I wanted to be dead, the thought of dying like that was enough to bring tears to my eyes. Please God, don't let Lucian Morelli be that evil.

Even Lucian Morelli couldn't be that evil.

Only he *could* be. Lucian Morelli could be the most evil monster I'd ever known.

I nearly cried with relief when I heard a car pull up the driveway and into the garage. I rushed up to the window but couldn't see anything, just pitch black outside. Nothing until the porch light came on and lit up the figure heading up to the front door.

I stepped back and pressed myself up against the wall, braced and ready. The front door slammed downstairs, and I heard footsteps. I heard movement.

It was him. I knew it was him.

I don't know whether I was more scared or more relieved as I waited for his entry. Only it didn't come. Nothing came.

More movement sounded downstairs but still nothing. Still no footsteps on the stairs.

It felt like I was waiting a lifetime, standing there with my heart thumping hard. When his footsteps finally did sound out on the stairs, I was almost grateful he was coming. Anything would be better than fading away alone.

The key was heavy in the lock. The door swung open slow and steady, and there he was. The huge frame of him was lit up by the light from downstairs.

He didn't speak to me, just stood there, leaning against the frame, even more sinister in his ease.

I didn't speak to him, because my throat was dry and I didn't know what the hell to say.

"It's late," he told me. "I don't have time for disobedience. And I sure as hell don't have the patience. Punishment will be severe if it's required."

I nodded, and he stepped back onto the landing, heading downstairs. My legs felt like jelly as I followed him. I really did feel like the little doll he expected me to be.

He was in the kitchen when I joined him. My eyes were blinking against the harshness of the light as they focused on the man before me. Yeah, he was Lucian Morelli at his finest. He was beautiful enough to take my breath away.

I didn't want to ask him for anything just in case that provoked him to deny it. I forced myself to stand there, waiting and hoping.

As it turns out, the monster had at least a sliver of kindness in his bones.

He handed me a mineral water, and I gulped it down in one.

"Thanks," I said, more bothered about basic necessities than the fact I was naked in some gleaming kitchen in front of a man who wanted to kill me.

I had no idea what time it was, but I knew it was late. The monster actually looked tired. Maybe even a little resigned. I'd never imagined seeing him like this.

He always looked so immortal.

I found my voice. "Guess something pretty urgent dragged you away."

"Not your business," he said back, deadpan.

We had another minute of silence. Heavy.

I wondered what he was planning on doing to me. Whether he'd make the pain harsh and hard, or slow and sensual. Maybe both.

I wondered whether he would finally get around to taking my virginity, and whether it would be as good as my fantasies promised before he tore me apart.

"Did you miss me?" he asked, his voice almost soft. Musical.

"No." But I was cold enough that my nipples were hard. His stare almost heated them as he looked me up and down. My thighs clenched tight together. He noticed. He could see plenty.

"I'm bored," he told me. "Time for you to entertain me."

I shrugged. "I'm bored too. Maybe it's time for you to entertain me right back."

I was coming to know his evil smirk so well. It made me shiver. "Don't worry, sweetheart. You'll be entertained."

He gestured through to the hallway, and I didn't argue. I stepped out ahead of him, turning instinctively into the lounge.

I didn't realize how close behind me he was until he pressed up against me and wrapped his arm around my neck.

"I want your pain, little doll."

I knew what was coming when he forced me down over the arm of the couch and took his belt from his pants. I didn't need to look at him behind me. I'd been in this position plenty of times before…waiting for the belt…the pain…the punishment.

I yelled out the hurt as the first lash landed, right across my ass cheeks.

He was skilled enough that he hit the same spot twice. Then three times. Then four.

I was skilled enough at taking it that my skin began to burn in the most amazing of ways, hips rocking as the pain morphed and turned into the strangest of pleasures.

Release.

It was release.

"This is your punishment for being disrespectful earlier," he told me, and I didn't protest, just took it. "You're going to have to learn to watch that pretty little mouth of yours."

Five. Six. Seven.

I was gasping, crying out with every lash.

Eight. Nine. Ten.

Tingling.

Eleven. Twelve.

Hurting.

Yes. I was hurting.

I wanted to be hurting.

I needed to be hurting.

I was still rocking from the pain when Lucian Morelli's thumb plunged deep inside my asshole, so dry and tight it hurt like hell. I cried out over and over again. He pulled out and circled my asshole. And then he fucked me with it, rough enough that I whimpered.

He replaced the belt with his palm, slapping me fast. The slaps were loud in the room, masking my cries. I felt like his doll now.

I *was* his doll now.

My breaths were gasping when he twisted me over and forced me onto my knees. His cock was waiting, my mouth was open.

I sucked Lucian Morelli's cock, staring up at him with wide eyes as he forced his way deep. He choked me, and I took it like a good girl. He made me retch over and over, but it didn't stop me from sucking him.

"Someone's taught you well," he said with a grunt.

He was right on that. I'd been taught well. Only it wasn't someone who'd taught me, it was many. I'd had many cocks forced down my throat in my life.

I felt the throbbing in his cock and knew what

was coming.

He pulled out of my mouth and worked his length above me, and I opened my mouth.

The first spurt of cum landed across my face. The rest was a perfect stream on my tongue. I didn't swallow, just stared up at him as he caught his breath.

That's when he saw them…my fingers between my legs.

"You're a horny little doll, aren't you, Elaine?"

I didn't stop rubbing my clit. My mouth was still open with his cum glistening on my tongue, and I rubbed my clit so fast I shuddered.

My ass was on fire, my nipples were straining, and my clit lit up like a flare, sparking.

I came on my knees with my monster's cum across my tongue, and he watched me. He watched me with his dark, evil eyes.

CHAPTER EIGHT

Lucian

I DIDN'T SLEEP, just sat and watched the girl curled up naked on the couch. She was dreaming, exhausted. She was the prettiest thing I'd ever seen.

Just a shame she was a fucking Constantine.

I knew the city would shake as the war over Elaine began. Constantines against the Power brothers would be quite a spectacle. I'd be an avid spectator.

Just so long as they didn't find out the kidnapper was me.

Then it would bring the Constantine wrath down on my family. I wasn't worried about myself, but my mother and sisters would be in danger. I could walk away from Morelli Holdings...maybe. But I couldn't live with myself if I brought actual harm to my family.

The sun was rising through the window when my phone started its usual round of bleeps and pings for the day. The Morelli empire was already awake, deals and trades galore springing up for their usual rounds. And for once in my life I wasn't among them.

I wasn't emailing or calling or reading papers in manila folders.

It was a strange and foreign peace.

It was light outside when I finally moved from my seat. The coffee machine was live and active when my little doll presented herself in the kitchen doorway.

She was scared and tired, a beautiful combination.

She didn't bother to ask for a coffee. No doubt she knew better than that.

I made myself one as she watched me, the sadistic part of me set to enjoy her thirst as she watched me drinking mine. I felt insane as I realized the sadistic part of me wasn't winning the battle. I already had a mug out for my little doll before I stopped myself. Fuck it. I made her one anyway. I didn't give her options, just handed one over, black, to match mine.

"Thanks," she said, and flashed me a rare, meek smile.

Fuck. She was such a natural temptress. "Turn around," I said.

She looked at me blankly before she realized what I wanted to see. She turned her back to me, her ass so beautifully marked, faint lines of bruising.

The sight made my cock twitch. I stepped up to her just as she was raising her coffee mug to her lips. My hot breath on her neck made her shudder.

"I'm going back to the city," I told her, like she deserved an explanation. "Don't even think about trying to escape this place. You'll get nowhere. I'm locking you up tight, and even if you did get out, I'm barely a few minutes from wiping out that friend of yours. You'd never save him in time."

She turned to me and pulled a scowl. "Yeah, I know. I do have a brain you know. You don't need to keep pointing out the obvious every thirty seconds."

My hand was on her tit in a flash, squeezing hard. "Are you going to behave yourself?"

She winced as I twisted her flesh. "That depends on what *behave myself* means."

I didn't actually know what behave meant in that instance. Part of me wanted her tied up naked to the bedframe upstairs, another part wanted to think of her drifting around the place, curious and needy. "I'm going to have so much fun leaving bruises on you," I told her, letting go of her flesh and hating how I was telling myself just as much as her. "I love to make you cry, because it's like I can feel something through you."

She stared at me. "You're absolutely fucking insane."

That made me smirk, and it made her smirk back.

I straightened myself up in the hallway mirror before taking my keys from the table. Elaine was sassy as she stood in front of me, hand on hip as she flashed me a grin despite the fresh marks on her tit. "Enjoy your day at the office, *honey*."

"Watch your fucking mouth," I told her, then stepped outside.

I'd make her pay for that later.

CHAPTER NINE

Elaine

I'VE ALWAYS BEEN a sneak as well as a liar.

Curious, my mother used to say, before she hated me. I would wander around the family home like a little wisp, exploring places when other people weren't looking.

I found my sister Vivian's diary under her bed when she was fifteen. I read about her crush on Roberto Henley from drama group and how he'd grope her after class. I read how she'd talk about naughty things with Rachel Weston at their sleepovers and how they'd plan who they would marry one day. I crept into my mom's room once and found she had…things in her bedside table drawer. I went through Tinsley's makeup collection and found she'd *borrowed* some of Mom's secret toys.

When Lucian left for a few hours to get supplies, it was time to assuage my curiosity.

I scoped the place out a little when I was sure he'd be well on the road back into New York City. I checked the external doors first. Both locked. Then the windows. Every window had a lock on it. Of course, I could have found something to smash my way through. But I didn't. I stared out of the window, checking out the shadows in the distance.

I felt like an invader as I made my way upstairs. I kept to the edge of the black metal staircase on tiptoes, like some kind of criminal. It didn't make a tiny bit of sense since the owner knew full well I'd be snooping my way around.

The landing made a creak that sounded loud. My room, or my *box* as Lucian put it, was small and dark, even with the daylight shining in. The bathroom was nice, but also small. There were barely any toiletries in the shower unit—just an expensive body wash and shampoo. I was surprised when I opened the mirrored cupboard above the sink. One solitary toothbrush and toothpaste in the holder. It was more casual than I was expecting, propped there neatly.

It was weird to think of it being in Lucian's mouth. It was weird to think of Lucian using it in his mouth. I couldn't imagine it—the Morelli monster doing something so basic.

The woman in me wanted to overstep my boundaries in this space when he wasn't looking, so I did it. I took Lucian Morelli's toothbrush and ran my tongue over the bristles. It gave me strange shivers. *Naughty.* It felt a lot less naughty when I used his toothbrush for what it was intended for, then stepped into the shower. The heat was a beautiful relief.

There was a towel over the rack. I wrapped myself up in it snug then headed back out onto the landing. I knew what was waiting for me—the ultimate for a curious girl like me.

Lucian Morelli's door was the one at the far end. Even his door felt more sinister somehow. More imposing.

It wasn't locked.

Perhaps that made him a fool, but it wasn't locked.

His bed was huge in the space. His wardrobe was plain wood but stocked at odds with the rest of the place. It was brimming with clothes, suits that looked insane against such a mediocre backdrop. They smelled of him. Grand. Imposing.

He had an old leather watch in his bedside drawer with some initials on the strap. His handwriting was cursive but masculine, almost calligraphic. It suited him. His pen was fountain and jet black. I scrawled a sample of the ink across my hand. I used to love writing when I was a little girl. At least the handwriting told me something about the man, because the text didn't. They were stock abbreviations and numbers, scribbled graphs, aborted sentences. It was the shorthand of a very intelligent, very calculating mind.

I felt bizarrely at home in Lucian's bedroom. I guess because it felt like a home, even in its sparse decor. I wondered just how much time he really spent here and whether anyone knew he ever came. I doubted that somehow.

I didn't put my panties or my dress back on from the night before.

Instead I pulled one of Lucian's designer shirts from the hanger. The black richness made me look pale in the mirror when I slipped it on. I liked wearing his shirt; it felt private. I felt close to him in the most mundane of ways. That felt bizarrely close—closer than I'd ever have imagined. In some ways even closer than having his cock in my ass or his breath in my face.

I wondered when I'd see him again. The thought was both terrifying and exciting, a combination I was fast becoming accustomed to.

People adapt quickly, don't they?

I helped myself to some soup, it's far from a fancy restaurant up in Maine. I made myself a coffee and settled down to a mindless show on the sleek TV that rolled down from the ceiling. I couldn't focus on it. I was on hyper-alert, heart racing at the thought of a car pulling up in the driveway.

When a car did pull up in the driveway, I leapt up from my seat, a wreck as the nerves ate me up alive.

The monster was silent as he stepped inside and cast his eyes on me. His eyes were as dark as I'd ever seen them. His jaw was as firm as I'd ever known. It was barely dark outside, so he must have come straight here, perhaps leaving before the customary five o'clock. Surprising. I'm sure my expression must have told him so.

"Enjoying my shirt, are you? Taking liberties already."

I ran my hands down the fabric as he watched me. "Better than an unwashed dress, thank you very much. Some liberties are there to be taken." I paused, holding my hands on my hips. "Did you expect me to wander around naked all day?"

His answer was simple and straight. "Yes."

I couldn't help but smirk. "Sure thing, right.

Think this is a fairy tale?"

His smirk was right back. "Hardly. There's no happy ever after here. More like a tragedy. You're the innocent girl who falls victim to the monster in human form."

"A monster who has a decent body wash in his shower at least. Thank you."

He was on the edge of laughing. I could see it. He didn't. He cast his jacket on the sofa and headed to the kitchen. I followed him in time to see him flick on the coffee machine. I hoped I'd get one. Manners, at least before he fucked me up for his pleasure.

I felt strangely human in his presence, which was ridiculous given that he was the greatest enemy I'd ever known, right from the day I was born.

"Show me your ass," he told me. "I want to see the marks."

I spun for him and lifted the shirt, and then my cheeky side found its strength some more. I shook my butt for him, shooting him a glance over my shoulder.

He was on me in seconds, arm around my throat as he slapped me hard on the ass. "There's a very fine line between a girl who finds her voice to amuse me and one who is asking for a fucking beating, Elaine."

I knew that. I managed to nod, and he dropped me.

My cheeky side shriveled to nothing as he returned to the coffee machine. This man was going to be the end of me, I needed to remember that. His amusement was nothing to me. *He* was nothing to me. Lucian Morelli was fuck all to my Constantine soul, he never would be. Not in the rest of my sorry lifetime.

"Get on your knees," he said.

Chapter Ten

Lucian

THE LITTLE DOLL on the floor transfixed me.

Her blue eyes were pools, deep with their secrets. The different shades of her butterfly beauty were siren calls, even in the sterile surroundings. She seemed at home here, even more than she'd seemed at home in opulence. It shouldn't have surprised me.

She was even more beautiful from that angle, staring up at me. I stepped up close enough to enjoy it. "Take my shirt off. Now."

Her fingers fumbled, impudence forgotten. She was visibly nervous.

I wanted to see her slip her hand between her thighs again without permission, but she didn't. She was silent and still. "You're lucky you're so pretty," I told her.

She stayed silent. It frustrated me how much I

wanted her attitude. Because I did. Part of me wanted her attitude. Part of me even *liked* it. Disgusting.

I punished her for it, dragging her up to her feet and slamming her down onto the counter, her tits pressed tight to the wood. I reached into the drawer and pulled out the metal spatula. I ran it up her thighs, teasing her before striking.

She whimpered. I loved her pain.

I made her squeal again and again and again. I yanked her head back by her silky blonde curls, hungry to see tears streaming down her pretty cheeks, but there were none. She wasn't crying.

"I'll make you sob for me," I snarled, but she smiled.

"Don't count on it, sir." Her smile wasn't rude. It was genuine. It lit up the pain in her eyes.

I knew it. She was a masochist as desperate for my wrath as she was for my mercy.

My cock was a beast in my pants, lost to the siren even more than the rest of me.

Her virginity was the biggest temptation of all, there for the taking. I was used to taking whatever I wanted, whenever I wanted it. I had been since I was a young boy learning from his father. I always clicked my fingers and got whatever I summoned. I cast my eyes on anything

I desired and it arrived at my feet. People, possessions, places. So why didn't I take her?

Why hadn't I taken her tight little pussy yet?

Fuck knows.

I hit her some more, and she moved with me, rocking those hips as she gasped. The endorphins flooded her—I could sense it. Gasps turned to moans, taking it. Wanting it.

She wanted it. Elaine Constantine wanted me to hurt her.

I forced her thighs apart and curled my fingers around to her pussy. Her clit was a toy in my grip. I twisted. It hurt to a whole different tune.

I wondered what it felt like.

I wondered what her ass felt like, already reddening in a beautiful shade.

"I know you like it," I told her.

I turned her to face me, giving her no warning before I slapped her tits hard enough to make her bite her lip and whimper. I loved the way they pinked.

"The men who played with you, did they teach you to be a true little masochist?"

She didn't answer, just stared.

"I asked you a question," I said. "The men who played with you, did they teach you to be a true masochist?"

"I'm not talking about it," she whispered. "I don't tell my secrets."

I twisted her tits, so rough she cried out.

Under normal circumstances, I would've taken what I wanted and hurt her until she spat those secrets right out at me, but there was a strange desire in me.

Something I hadn't felt before.

I didn't want her spilling those secrets when I was beating her so bad she couldn't resist me. I wanted her whispering in the darkness with tears streaming down her cheeks, broken right down to the soul. I wanted her whispering her secrets like a good girl because she wanted to. Right to the core of her. Because she wanted to whisper them to *me*.

My brain was fucking me up, and I knew it. Sirens drown sailors for a fucking reason.

"You'll pay for your denial," I growled, and I meant it.

She knew it. She arched her back, presenting those perfect tits for more punishment.

She got it. Twists and slaps that had her eyes closed tight, struggling not to buckle and cry. Her struggling worked. She was resilient.

I guess she'd learnt to be. I guess they taught her to be. The thought of men teaching her to be resilient both enraged me and excited me in one, and always had done…only now the balance was shifting. Slowly, it was shifting. The rage was rising like venom behind my eyes.

"Please, Lucian, will you fuck me?" she asked. "Please fuck me."

I forced her onto her knees so hard she cried out. "I'll fuck your impudent little mouth until you vomit on my cock," I snarled. "I'll fuck your throat until you're nothing but a gasping little wreck on the floor. Is that what you want? That's what you're going to get."

Chapter Eleven

Elaine

I've never had much praise for being a good girl.

My father was nice enough, but he rarely had time for me.

My mother was cold, always focusing on criticism.

My sisters were better behaved than me. I was the black sheep.

I blamed myself for all the dirty attention I got. *You've been bad,* they used to tell me, *take your punishment like a good girl.* Maybe even from a young age, I believed them. Maybe they knew I would. *Maybe, maybe, maybe.* None of that mattered anymore.

I guess that's why I was proud that Lucian Morelli wanted me to suck his cock. He might hate me, but he didn't hate the way I flicked my tongue so perfectly up and down the length of him. His curses under his breath were anything but full of rage, and his fingers in my hair were desperate and not full of spite.

Yes, I was proud. I was proud of being such a good girl at sucking cock.

My tits were still hurting, but there was a tenderness about them that lit me up all the way through my body. My ass was still smarting, but that didn't make a difference to how good my clit was feeling as I stared up at the monster and how much he was enjoying my throat.

I should hate every single vein in his body, retching at the Morelli name as much as I was retching with his thrusts. But I wasn't hating it. I was tingling so hard I couldn't stop it.

"Take it," he growled, and I knew exactly what he wanted.

I opened my mouth nice and wide and stared up at him. Only this time he didn't give me his cum in my mouth. He wrenched my head back and spurted his load over my pinked tits, splattering them in thick cream.

He looked for long moments before casting me down onto my back. "Don't even think of hiding yourself," he told me. "You'll keep those filthy tits on display as long as I want them."

I didn't bother arguing, just remained kneeling as his cum cooled on my heated skin.

Lucian Morelli surprised me in no time as he got himself busy in the refrigerator. I was still gazing up at him as he assembled cheeses and salami and pasta from the cupboard. The beast of the Morelli family was preparing food. I'd never have pictured the beast of the Morelli family making food.

He must have caught sight of my shock.

"Don't be dumb and think this is kindness on my part. If I trusted you for a second to make me anything even vaguely passable, I'd be using you as my chef as well as my sex doll."

"I can cook spaghetti," I scoffed, offended. "And grilled cheese."

He didn't punish me for my attitude, not this time. Strangely I supposed we were getting used to each other somehow—two mortal enemies holed up in a small space who didn't seem to be all that different in many ways, despite our world of opposites.

He didn't protest when I got to my feet, cum still splattered thick on my tits. I propped against the counter, watching him. His hands were surprisingly skilled with the meal preparation, and I knew even more of his familiarity in the space by the way he was so at ease with the kitchen. Not only could Lucian Morelli cook a meal, but he seemed to be plenty accustomed to it. Definitely more accustomed to it than I was. He was right on that front.

"You'd better be grateful and eat what's put in front of you," he told me. "I'm feeding you to keep that body of yours fit for my playtime, not because I give a fuck about your hunger."

A tiny part of me didn't believe him. That tiny part of me was probably a fool, but I didn't believe him. He wasn't just feeding my body, he was feeding me, too.

It didn't take him long to spoon pasta into a bowl and hand it over. He stalked on through to the dining room and set himself down at the table. I didn't say a word as I sat down alongside him and picked at the meal with my fork. It was good, actually.

The monster could cook.

I couldn't hold back my sarcasm, not giving a fuck for how my ass was throbbing against the wood of my chair. "So, how was your day, sweetheart?" I asked him with a sarcastic tone.

He shot me a glare that made my heart leap. "It was made all the better for hearing about the wreck your disappearance has caused. Your family's going to war with the Power brothers. I can't wait to see the bloodshed and the pain when they truly come to battle."

I got a flutter in my chest. Guilt as well as curiosity. Why would my family go to war with the Power brothers? My mother had already refused to bail me out. Then again, maybe it was for show. A thing about Constantine pride. I never understood pride.

"Everyone seems convinced it's the Power brothers. I suppose your deep, dark secrets of a large debt weren't exactly secret."

If only he knew.

If only he knew just how many secrets naughty little Elaine really kept from the world.

I didn't say a word about them, just used the opportunity for more criticism.

"You won't be so cocky when the world comes to realize just what you've done here. Even your own family will destroy you. There's no way Bryant Morelli is going to tolerate you being with me."

"You know fuck all about the Morelli family."

In that moment, I came to regret just how my frantic action to point the finger at the Power brothers saved the monster's skin, at least for the time being.

I only hoped he'd never find out before they killed him. That, or before he killed me.

I'd never want to handle that shame and embarrassment in front of him, to have to explain why I saved him instead of turning him over to my family's wrath.

"Push the fucking boundaries all you like. I'll make you suffer for all of them. But believe me, you choose to use your pretty little tongue against the Morelli name, and I'll cut the snark right out of you."

I shut my mouth with a nod and carried on eating, but Lucian Morelli was lying to himself. There's no way he'd cut my tongue from my mouth before he killed me—not when it played his cock so well. His defense of the Morelli family name felt different this time. More strained. As if he had bigger priorities than a feud that had consumed our families for decades.

Chapter Twelve

Lucian

ELAINE WAS SHAKY as I forced her into her box that night. She was still naked, with those sweet tits on display. She was the perfect doll. She shot me a look from inside the room, big eyes fixing on mine with a *please* she didn't say. *Please don't leave me here.*

She didn't want to be alone.

Part of me didn't want to leave her alone. I wanted her next to me, subject to my every whim, whenever I wanted it. Still, I couldn't share a bed with a Constantine. Or with my little doll. I couldn't stoop that low, even by my current standards of jackass insanity.

"Make sure you sleep," I told her. "I want that body perfect for me tomorrow."

She didn't reply, and no doubt the exhaustion won out in her. She slipped into bed and pulled the covers up high. She curled into a fetal position before I closed the door on her, and it was…strange. It gave me a weird feeling I couldn't place. Almost like pain.

I shut the door firmly and headed away.

My bed was a large floating structure in the center of a large bedroom. I wanted Elaine to entertain me, but instead I made plans for her. Plans to hurt, stretch, push to the ultimate limit, and I jerked off to the thrill of all the good things to come.

Sleep found me then, as always, it found me.

Elaine was already awake when I set foot outside my room, showered and dressed the next morning. She was in the kitchen making herself a coffee like she owned the damn place. It gave me another one of those weird pricks of a feeling to see she had another mug waiting on the counter, ready to pour. One for me.

"Uncomfortable bed?" I asked her. "Be grateful I gave you one at all."

"Most beds are uncomfortable to me," she said, "I've had a lifetime of bad experiences, staring at the door, scared of who's going to come in and climb on my bed."

"I'll be the one climbing on your damn bed."

She cast a glance at my suit and the keys already in my hand. "Heading into the office? Should I be a good 1950s wife and cook green bean casserole while you're gone?"

"No, sweetheart. You're my little doll. And good little dolls move their limbs back and forth, they brush their hair, they shave the hair from their bodies so they're smooth and ready."

"Gross." She poured me a coffee and held it out to me. "At least drink this before you hit the road. You hardly want to be driving without any caffeine in you."

I stared at her puzzled, nothing short of shocked, because it couldn't possibly…it couldn't possibly be Elaine Constantine *caring*.

She seemed to register my confusion; it hit her as strangely as it hit me. Her justification was instant.

"It's about your body, not you," she said. "What's going to happen to me if you get in a car crash and don't come back? I'll starve after a while. Fuck you, by the way."

She went to take the coffee back, but I grabbed it from her. I'd been raised with solid manners, and they couldn't hold back. The words were out of me before I could stop them. "Thank you."

Elaine was taken aback by that too. I knew she

was fighting the response, but we couldn't stop it. Even in our hate, we couldn't stop it. "You're welcome," she said with another shrug, then added the obligatory, "You're welcome, asshole."

"Have you any damn idea how ridiculously immature you sound when you use that term?" I asked her. "You sound like a rebellious child." I downed my coffee. She'd done a good job of it.

"I'll be wearing one of your shirts today," she told me. "You can punish me for it when you get home all you want, but I'll still be wearing it."

There it was again, another ridiculous statement. *Home*. When you get *home*.

"When you get *back*," she followed up, but it was too late.

"This isn't my fucking *home*," I said. "It's a dungeon where I'm torturing you until you scream. Don't for a second think I'm *home* here."

"Torturing me until I scream? That's all? What about blood and despair? What about torturing me until I black out? Don't tell me you're going soft in your old age." She lifted her smirking jaw to me. My free hand shot to her exposed throat and fucking squeezed.

"Maybe you don't deserve to black out."

"Do it," she choked out.

I let go of her throat and forced my fingers

into her gasping mouth, shunted her backwards as she gargled her own spit and retched against me. Retched until it ran down her nostrils and her eyes watered as I twisted my fingers into her throat.

When I pulled my hand free, she doubled over, gasping as her drool puddled on the floor.

"Get that shit cleaned up before I get back," I told her, only just resisting the urge to fuck her up some more.

"Whatever," she said as I walked away and caught sight of the time on the clock above the counter, her voice hoarse.

Fucking hell, I was later than even I'd expected.

I was never late...not before Elaine Constantine became my little doll.

The car was waiting in the garage and so was the road ahead, all damn sixty minutes of it.

I knew what was looming—Seamus and Duncan and their lowlife attempts at kissing Father's backside. They could go fuck themselves.

Sure enough they were hovering when I arrived in my office at Morelli Holdings. Seamus was on his phone trying to sound as slick and professional as possible, and Duncan was flicking through paperwork he had no right to be flicking through. I snatched it from him as soon as I was in reaching distance.

"Get the fuck out of my office."

The man had the audacity to laugh at me. "It's not your office. It's your *daddy's*. He knows we're here this morning. He also knows you weren't."

Fuck's sake.

"I'll be handling my father," I told them both with a snarl. "Believe me, you have no place here, and you'll be getting the fuck out of my building."

It was Seamus who laughed this time, dropping his phone onto my desk.

"You'd better go handle him then, shouldn't you? He's downstairs on floor nine." He tutted like a prick. "Believe *me,* he's not a happy daddy this morning."

Somehow I knew the assholes were telling the goddamn truth and it was a ball ache. Under any normal circumstances I would've put it down to my own fucking around in Bishop's Landing and not at Holdings where I belonged. And nothing else. My fucking bad.

My gut knew a whole lot more than that when I headed downstairs to floor nine, though. My gut had more sense than my goddamn fucking brain. Father's presence in the office wasn't just about fucking around in Bishop's Landing and slacking at Holdings—this was about Elaine fucking Constantine. I knew it in my veins. The whole world was going Elaine Constantine crazy, not just me. I'd heard it all over the news on the way in.

Kidnapped. Somehow the whole damn world knew she'd been kidnapped.

I arrived on floor nine, and I almost regretted taking her from her sorry apartment in the first place. I almost wished I would've left her to the Power brothers and her own pitiful family to fuck up, that or kill herself and save everyone else the bother.

Almost. Jesus Christ, I only registered my thoughts as I stepped into the meeting room. *Almost* wished I'd left her? What the fuck was happening to me?

One thing was for sure, Father would be damned certain he was going to find out.

Chapter Thirteen

Elaine

URNING ON THE TV in the morning and seeing your face staring out at you from every channel is a weird experience—weird enough to make you jump from your seat. There I was, staring out at me from the screen in Lucian Morelli's countryside shack, featuring on every news broadcast.

Elaine Constantine kidnapped!

How the hell did the news stations know I'd been kidnapped?

Wow, I was getting good coverage. It was official, I'd been kidnapped. Hello there, media shitstorm. The police were involved. If only they knew I was kidnapped by a Morelli, news would reach a whole new stratosphere.

People were speculating on every station, talking about sicko freaks in the world who may have taken me. That's when it was getting crazy. There were random people talking about how they'd seen me places—dingy nightclubs alongside Tristan. *Fuck.*

Maybe they might start talking about Lucian being in those places too.

I almost enjoyed sitting on the couch in Lucian's shirt watching my drama unfold on the screen. It was bizarrely exciting somehow, feeling so important to the world outside.

Tinsley was there, crying and asking for anyone to give information. No doubt Mom had drafted her in to play the part of the heartbroken sister after a heinous kidnapping.

There was no mention of the Power brothers or my debt, at least in the media. But in the Constantine universe it was undoubtedly them who'd taken me. They'd have figured that out regardless, but not to the same extent as they would have done once they'd barged into my room that night and looked for the answers. I can't believe I really supported the fact that the Power brothers had taken me. I was embarrassed at the thought Lucian would find out about that…about the note…the note I'd…I'd scribbled…

Fuck.

I stepped away from the TV as I made myself a coffee and soup, feeling more at home in that smooth space than I ever felt in my own apartment. I wished in some ways that Lucian would just bail out on me for good and leave me to enjoy my life here without everyone around me. Hell, I was almost wishing I could stay *alive*, despite the constant regular shit of wanting my days to end I'd been carrying around with me for years.

But no.

No.

Lucian Morelli wasn't my friend. And this wasn't a sanctuary.

It was a clue as to just how fucked up my head was when I started looking at the clock, wondering when Lucian would be back, if at all. That broken girl in me was almost hoping he would come back soon and shove more than his fingers down her throat. That broken girl needed to hurt. Needed her damn punishment.

That broken girl was too messed up for a reason.

Lunchtime came and went slowly, and even the TV stations stopped holding my interest. Hearing about what a lovely girl I was on screen was a joke when I'd been hearing what a bad one I was for decades. I switched it off with a curse, and then I sat there, bored.

I tried again and watched another load of random speakers speculating where I was on the TV, and still I was bored.

That's when the boredom turned, just like it always did. Boredom turned into mind-wandering memories, and they turned dark quickly without cocaine or alcohol to numb me. Memories that chewed me up inside.

I could feel them brewing, just like always. Feel them reaching out at me from the pits of my own fucked-up soul, just like always.

I heard them, felt them, feared them.

No, please. I'll be a good girl. I promise I'll be a good girl.

Don't touch me again. Please, don't touch me like that. Don't make it hurt.

It hurts, Uncle Lionel, please don't let them in tonight. Please!

My desperate sense of desire drove me back to the kitchen. I opened the drawer with trembling fingers, knowing what was coming, knowing what I needed, knowing what I *always* needed.

The knives were sharp.

I picked the one Lucian had used so well for the salami the night before. I ran it over my thumb to check it, and it was good enough. Sharp enough. It would cut me just fine.

Dear Lord, if only those memories would fuck off and die instead of me. I sat down with my back to the cupboard, taking deep breaths as I prepared myself. There was no point denying the obvious, those memories kept on coming. Eating me up.

Please, don't touch me like that!

I nicked my thigh, just enough to feel the sting.

Please, Uncle Lionel, please. Don't let them!

The next cut was longer, deeper.

Please, no. No. Not there!

Blood. Enough blood that I could feel the release.

I'll be a good girl, just don't hurt me, please!

My thighs were dripping. The rush of pain and relief soothed me.

I'll be a good girl and put you in my mouth. I'll be a good girl and put my hand between my legs.

I tipped my head back against the cupboard and enjoyed the sensation. Fresh cuts on scars. Lucian would punish me for them, but I didn't care. I would welcome that punishment, remember my manners and thank him for it.

If only I was brave enough to slit my wrists and set myself free, but I wasn't. I'd never been brave enough to do that. If I would've been brave enough to do that I would've already been dead when Lucian Morelli came for me that night.

If only I'd been sane enough to want to damn Lucian Morelli to a hell of his own, then I'd never have left the note about the Power brothers on my kitchen counter.

Chapter Fourteen

Lucian

ELAINE WAS A butterfly with wings of so many wonderful fucked-up colors they could blind a man if he looked too deep. I didn't understand her. I shouldn't want to.

She shouldn't transfix me.

I was back in the car like a man possessed before I could stop myself as the day reached its close, heading out alongside everyone with a regular day job, even though I'd already faced the wrath from my father.

"What the fuck is happening to you, Lucian? Why are you abandoning Holdings?"

Ironic, to get a call from my father.

He was worried. I could hear it in his voice. He liked to play the game. The power struggle. The coup. He enjoyed it, but he never thought I'd stop playing.

It was *his* truth to share with me that had my senses reeling beyond all recognition.

Elaine Constantine told her family directly that it was the Power brothers waiting for her outside. By letter. She told them by letter. A hand scrawled letter on her kitchen counter.

So I know you didn't do this. I'm relieved, because I know you had a…well, a fascination with her. But let me tell you, father to son, man to man, that you're better off without her. Forget her. Come back to the company. You won't be the CEO, but you were never going to win.

My course of action was clear and determined as I pulled up into my driveway at Bishop's Landing. I was going to find out what the fuck Elaine was thinking with that letter. I was going to take that sweet little virgin pussy of hers as mine while she confessed her secrets.

I was expecting a presentation of her usual impudence as soon as I stepped over the threshold, but she wasn't parading around the place. She wasn't in the hallway and she wasn't in the living room, even though the TV was still blaring out with her face on the screen. I had a flash of panic that she'd smashed a window and gotten away.

But she was in the kitchen, and the sight of her caught my breath—sitting down on the floor with her knees up to her chest, lost to the world around her.

That sharp prick got me again, in the gut this time. The one I hated, the one that made no sense to me, the one that was all about Elaine Constantine.

I yanked her up to her feet, slamming her into the counter like a piece of meat ready for the slaughter. Only that's when she caught my breath again, that's when I finally saw the streaks of tears down her pretty cheeks and realized what they were for.

The blood was crusty on her thighs, cuts still raw from where she'd butchered herself. I should've loved it, her pain, her blood, her tears, but I didn't. The thought of anyone hurting her flesh that wasn't me, even herself, was enough to slam me with rage.

"What the fuck is this? What the fuck do you think you were doing?"

This time there wasn't even a spark of spite in her as she stared up at me. She was a broken girl, lost to every hurt and fear in the world.

I bent down to retrieve the knife from the floor. She'd picked the best, clearly determined for the cleanest slices. She flinched as I slammed it down onto the counter.

"If you'd left me alcohol, I wouldn't need to."
She was shaking, clearly wallowing in her own shit
and unable to get a grip of it. There they were,
peeping through the surface—those intoxicating
little butterfly secrets. The colors of pain and rage
and grief that intoxicated me.

"Or maybe I'll just lock up the knives."

Her eyes got their venom back at that point.
Her jaw tightened. "Fuck you, Morelli! You have
no fucking idea how damaged I am. Go fuck
yourself!"

"No, I don't," I said. "But I'll find out. Those
secrets inside you will be mine for the taking. I
can't wait to find out just how damaged you really
are."

"Don't count on it," she said. "I'm not telling
you shit."

She tried to pull away, but I wouldn't let her.
I pressed up against her with my hands on either
side of the countertop. She was pinned. Con-
tained. *Mine.*

I laughed. "Clearly, you don't hate me nearly
so much as you hate your own family, sweetheart.
Them or the Power brothers it seems. You must
have a secret dirty liking for the Morellis, seeing
how you set the Power brothers up for *my* crime."

"I don't know what the fuck you're talking

about, asshole." She was lying. We both knew it.

"It seems you wrote a damning little letter, didn't you?" I whispered with spite. "A scrawled little note to tell the world you'd been taken by the Power brothers."

She tried to lie some more. "I just wanted them to take some shit for all the hell they put me through. I just wanted them to suffer."

I gave her an evil smile. "Oh, really? You hate the Power brothers more than the Morellis?"

She didn't try to lie again. She just stared, hating me.

I leaned even closer to taunt her. "I'd even dare to say you hate your own family more than the Morellis, don't you? Maybe you aren't worthy of the Constantine name."

"I'm damn well worthy of the fucking Constantine name," she snarled at me, and then she found a flare of life in the depths of her. She twisted between my arms like a snake, scrabbling against the counter to reach for the blade, and then she grabbed it. She grabbed it and let out a screech as she plunged it straight through my hand. "Fuck you, Morelli."

That's when she should have run like a crazy thing and tried to get the fuck out of there. She tried to, really she did. She made to run, but I was still holding her tight.

I was smiling. Smirking. Loving just how horrified she was when she saw I didn't flinch in the slightest. My hand was bound to the wood of the counter, and I didn't even let out a curse.

Elaine was so shocked that she drained white when I pulled the blade free of my hand and cast it straight back onto the counter.

"What the fuck?!" she spat. "What the fuck is wrong with you? I just sliced right through your fucking hand, Lucian! Are you out of your mind?"

My laugh was every bit as evil as she'd ever known.

Chapter Fifteen
Elaine

I COULDN'T MOVE, staring in shock and horror at the way Lucian pulled the knife out of his hand. He didn't flinch, didn't falter, didn't express even a moment of pain. I stared at him as he wrapped his bleeding hand in a towel. He'd said the words, but I didn't believe them, not until I saw it with my own eyes. Not until I felt his flesh give way, skin and tendon sliced, even while I looked into his eyes. He didn't even flinch.

"What the fuck," I managed to whisper.

A chuckle. "What the fuck is right with me, more like it."

I still didn't fathom it. I couldn't. His hand was already bleeding through the towel but he didn't give a fuck. "Is this the pain thing you were talking about?"

His eyes were as dark as ever as he answered me. "Congenital insensitivity to pain. Nothing you ever do will hurt me. If you have any sense in that pretty head of yours, you'll abandon all hopes of it now and do whatever the fuck you're told."

"Nothing will hurt you? For real? Nothing?"

"That's the side effect of my little disorder. I can't feel it. If I have my hand on the stove, it will burn to a crisp. I won't feel a thing. Only the smell will make me notice."

This was huge. Everyone would know if the Morelli heir couldn't feel pain. It would be part of the gossip. Part of the jokes. Part of the oeuvre of being rich and powerful in New York.

"I'm supposed to be able to feel emotional pain, but I never have. So in that way I've never felt pain at all. Which is quite ironic. Quite unfair. Proof that there isn't a just God. Because I can feel pleasure just fine. I can fuck and enjoy myself just fine."

He couldn't feel pain? Not physical, he said. Not even emotional pain. Not yet anyway. I hoped some woman would eventually stomp his heart to pieces. But he could feel pleasure. No wonder he stormed through life, taking everything he wanted, throwing everything else back.

The monster's eyes were so cold, but there was

a hint of something else in his gaze, some kind of unlikely vulnerability in his darkness. People would have talked about Lucian Morelli having congenital insensitivity to pain if they had known.

How had they kept this a secret? Who in the family knew about it?

"Is this why you hurt people so much?" I asked him. "Because you have no idea what it feels like? Maybe if you did, you wouldn't be such a bastard to people."

"I don't need an excuse to be a bastard to people, don't try to make one for me."

I leaned back against the counter. "I wasn't going to. You can't excuse being that much of a sadistic asshole with a damn illness."

We stood staring, eye to eye, both of us hating each other, both of us curious, both of us in so much of a fucked-up state we must have been in some surreal dimension in Constantine-Morelli hell.

I guess my tone was genuine when it sounded out next, because I saw his eyes lighten just a touch. "What do the doctors say about it? Can it be fixed?"

"I didn't want to be fixed."

"Why not?" I asked.

"Because pain is a weakness, Elaine. I'm free

of it. I'm stronger for it."

I didn't believe him. Pain was a truth and a connection to yourself. Pain was something that made us stronger, not weaker. "Is it something you've had your whole life?"

"From when I was young enough to scrape my knees and not cry along with it."

I could only begin to imagine the little toddler Lucian with bleeding legs, not needing to cry for his mom. "Who else knows?" I pushed. "People must know, right?"

"None of your business," he told me, but I shook my head.

"Seriously, Lucian. You can't tell me it's none of my business. I just stabbed you through the hand, and you're telling me you didn't feel it. How could that never have come up before?"

"People see what they want to see. You should know that. They look at you and see a party girl. They don't know that you're a virgin. Or that you're absolutely terrified."

"You are an interesting piece of shit, Lucian Morelli, even if I can't stand you."

I knew he was trying to hide a laugh at my bold words. Sometimes I definitely made him laugh inside, no matter how much he wanted to hate me. "Forget about it," he said. "Believe me, you'll be paying for your actions badly enough already."

I didn't give a shit about that. I was more interested in the weird creature in front of me than I was in what he was going to do with me.

I wondered if the rest of his family had it too. The question was out of my mouth before I'd even realized I was saying it. "Who else around you has it? Nobody talks about you guys having it."

He walked away far enough to flick the coffee machine on, the intensity of the mood broken. His sigh felt casual, almost affectionate. "Stop asking questions, little doll."

I didn't want to shut my mouth, I wanted to know every little bit of his secrets. I was like the sneaky little girl tiptoeing through everyone else's mysteries all over again, *curious.* "I can hear your brain ticking," he told me. "Forget it."

My brain sure was ticking. "Even the Morellis don't know, do they? You didn't tell anyone?"

He poured a coffee, and I waited quietly as he took a sip of his drink, wondering just what other secrets his body was holding tight. Maybe we were both creatures of secrets. Maybe there was more in common between us than I would've ever believed.

I watched him, trying to understand. I tried to imagine what it must be like in a body like his, so perfect but so oblivious to pain. What must it be like to watch everyone around you crying out when things hurt them, but not having a clue how on earth that could feel?

I got a shiver as I began to realize just what that might mean for a man like Lucian…just what that could lead to…such natural sadism…this natural need to hurt people…

"So that's why, isn't it? That's why you're such a fucking psycho?"

Another sigh. "Shut your mouth or I'll shut it for you."

He sounded tired.

He was fixated on causing people pain…and he would be…of course, he would be…he'd be fixated on causing people pain because he had none of his own…

"It makes you a sadist, doesn't it?"

"Sadism doesn't need a reason, sweetheart. We aren't broken men for you to fix. I hurt you because I'm a bastard who likes seeing you in pain. What does it matter, the reason why?"

His stare made me shudder when it landed on me again—a whole load of layers glistening through the surface, like a moth in the darkness with the faintest of color in his pitch black wings.

CHAPTER SIXTEEN

Lucian

I WAS A private person by nature. Having to keep my secret made it worse.

And being the son of Bryant Morelli... well, that sealed the deal. Any weaknesses as a boy were chased out of me by my father. The Morelli heir had to be a monster of utter perfection.

Still, despite my lifetime of privacy, part of me wanted to tell Elaine my history. I wanted to see the shock in her pretty eyes as I told her the complete Lucian Morelli story.

I wanted to see her open mouth as I told her about the very early days when Father noticed my insensitivity to pain, and how he'd tested my limits with his gritted jaw.

"Can you feel this, boy? Tell me when it hurts..."

His hand, then his belt, then the nasty cuts.

The way he twisted my flesh and held me down and thumped me hard enough that it sent me flying.

I didn't feel a thing.

Part of me wanted to. I wanted to know what it felt like to have my body so abused and broken.

He took me to the doctor, and then a specialist after him, with the threat of death if they so much as recorded my results. Their reply was quick and definite. Congenital insensitivity to pain.

My body had no concept of what hurting meant.

Father told me that it would be a sin against the Morelli name to tell a soul about my condition, even my mother. He told me that he'd be ashamed of me forever if I breathed a word of it to anyone in this world. So I didn't tell them. I didn't tell my mother, or my brothers and sisters, or any of my *friends* at school. I didn't tell my teachers, didn't explain a word to them why I didn't ever cry out in sports matches when somebody crashed right into me.

It was none of their business. Nothing about me was anyone's business.

I don't remember how old I was when other people's pain began to fascinate me.

Everyone's pain began to fascinate me, but I had a particularly strong taste for pretty girls with big, crying eyes. Maybe I was twelve or thirteen. I'd long grown to rule the schoolyard by slamming my punishment out on anyone I chose, but that was mainly on other boys—rivals and losers alike. Big for my age, I enjoyed going after older boys and making them suffer.

The first girl I hurt was Bethany Fryers. I was fourteen years old. She was walking through the park after art class one day with a spring in her step, blonde hair swinging as she walked. I'd noticed her before, her gaze on me. Curious. A little intimidated.

My mouth watered at the sight of her, and my cock hardened like I'd known it to do at night for years. I had such a strong need to see her beg me to stop that it took my breath away. So I asked her to take a walk with me. And there in the bathroom of the school, I fucked her in a dirty stall. She didn't mind spreading her legs but her eyes got wide when I covered her mouth. She squirmed in pain when I twisted her nipples. But she was wet and bucking against me. She wanted it.

I hurt her where nobody else would see it. I unbuttoned her blouse and saw her pretty nipples there, and something made me want to hurt them worse than anything else. I did hurt them. I twisted them so hard in my fingers that she whimpered, and her whimper thrilled me. It felt private somehow. Her shallow little breaths made me feel like more of a god than I'd ever known.

Instinct takes over, even at that age. Biting her felt like the most natural thing in the world. I loved the marks I left on her, so pink against her skin. I knew they would bruise and hurt her later as well as in the moment. I wanted to hurt her over and over again just to keep those marks alive on her skin.

She was older than me, probably fifteen. Her tits were a lovely shape that jiggled just right when I slapped them. It was my first fuck, and I didn't hold back.

"Ahhh, owww. Owww. Lucian, please…"

Only it wasn't just a cry of pain as I squeezed her and pulled her nipples. There was more in her eyes as she arched her back for me, even as she was whimpering…and then that whimpering changed to a different type of whimper.

She came from nothing more than my violence on her skin, her mouth open as she moaned for me. That was power.

"You come back here next week," I said, referring to our next art class. "I want to see what these bruises look like. And I'm going to fuck you again."

She knew that I'd be waiting for her, in exactly the same spot at exactly the same time.

She didn't fight me, because she knew there would be no point. What's more, she wanted what I dished out, wanted it so badly she never strayed from that exact path. She was meek as she followed me down the bank to our usual spot, spreading herself wide open so I could hurt her however I wanted.

Bethany Fryers was the first girl I fucked.

She was the first girl I fucked so hard it hurt her, and that thrilled me more than ever.

I was like a demon possessed as I hunted down other pretty girls I wanted to be inside of, and I found them. Found the ones who craved the sort of pain I dished out, needed it so much they'd beg me for it. I found so many of them, I lost count through the years.

Father knew about it. I think eventually one of the girls' daddies found out about what I was doing and confronted him at Morelli Holdings.

I was scared shitless as he walked into my room one evening with that dangerous look in his eyes. I knew he knew. I could see it before he said a word.

I wondered what he was going to do to punish me, seeing as his belt would make no difference whatsoever, not like it did with my brothers. As it turns out, he didn't punish me. He sat down on the bed next to me with a strange smile on his face.

"I always knew you'd be a strong boy," he said to me. "Believe me, Lucian, it's a good thing. You need to be strong in this family. I'm proud of you, Son."

With that he was gone, and he never mentioned it again.

It didn't matter how many people I hurt, or how many girls I touched, or how many boys I beat up until I was their ruler—he never mentioned it again.

Neither had I. Other than forging the Violent Delights club with Clark Ventana and signing Rex Halloway up for my virgin purchases, and Trenton Alto knowing way more about me than he should, I hadn't spilled my truths to anyone.

So why the holy fuck was I tempted to spill my truths to Elaine Constantine?

Chapter Seventeen

Elaine

MY INSIDES WERE going crazy with nerves and flutters. That curiosity I knew so well was going wild inside me, desperate to know just what Lucian Morelli was hiding from the world.

He was quiet and brooding as he made another coffee, his hand still bleeding into the towel. I wondered if he needed a doctor for stitches, but he didn't seem bothered in the slightest, and his hand seemed to be working just fine.

I didn't push him, didn't speak, just let him churn in his darkness. The thrill and hope was already burning deep inside me that maybe, just maybe, he'd tell me something. Anything. Just something to give my curiosity one little tickle.

"If you stab anyone in the hand again," he finally said, "you want to make sure you do it more centrally. You barely cut more than skin."

If. *If* I stab anyone in the hand. Like I was ever going to see anyone. I nodded at him. "Sure thing. I guess I'm a crappy hand stabber. My bad."

He smirked, unable to hide the amusement, even though I'd just sliced him open. "You have such an impudent little tongue on you, Elaine," he said. "Some people might even find it funny."

Some people like *him*, even if he didn't want to admit it.

Still I kept quiet, letting him churn, letting him think. I couldn't even imagine what went on inside a mind like Lucian's. He was such a different creature to me that the very idea of the life inside of him must be like an alien planet. Or maybe the depths of hell.

I pretended not to care so much about what he might tell me, but it was a pointless exercise, I'm sure it was blatantly obvious that I was desperate to know. My thighs were still sore from the places I'd sliced them, but I didn't give a crap about that anymore. I didn't feel the need for that anymore. All I needed was the words of the monster in front of me as he sipped his coffee.

"It's a power," he told me after another minute of pure silence. "I'm immune to every pain that people want to dish out to me. I don't have to worry about anything they might dish out. They either kill me or mean nothing."

That's an interesting thought. *They either kill me or mean nothing.* I could see how that was a form of power. I wished I could feel that way. "You must wonder about pain though."

I thought he was going to tell me to *mind my own fucking business*, but he didn't. He fixed me with that piercing stare of his and put his mug on the counter. "Of course. I enjoy the thrill of watching people in pain. Especially you."

"I guess I would too," I said with a shrug, and he pulled a face at me.

"You think you'd be a sadist, do you, if you didn't know pain?"

I pulled a face right back at him. "No, probably not. I'd probably not be a sick fuck like you, but I'm sure I would be curious. I'm curious about everything."

Another smirk from him. "Clearly you're curious. If you weren't overly curious you'd have the sense to shut your mouth."

I dared to push him, just a little. "When did you find out? You must have been young."

I wasn't expecting him to actually answer me. The facts were simple enough. The pain tolerance. But I was in shock when he told me just how much of a little boy he was and how his father had pushed his body for the truth. No wonder Lucian Morelli was so twisted, he'd been fucked up from one hell of an early age.

He pulled another face when he registered how my mind was working. "He didn't fucking abuse me, Elaine. He was finding out who I was."

I didn't agree with him but didn't voice it.

"You have no idea how much power it gave me, knowing just how immune I was to hurt."

"I have an idea how much power it gave you," I told him. "Considering just how much you've used it to get your own way and bully people into submission every moment of your life. It's just a shame you've never actually done things with people because they want to, not because you bully them."

"That's not true in the slightest. I've done plenty of things with people because they want to."

I could see him thinking about it, trying to work out when that was, and it made me smile at him. "Don't worry, Lucian, you don't have to justify yourself to me. Bully people all you want. It's just a shame. I'm *sure* plenty of people would do things with you just because they wanted to." I couldn't resist turning the knife even though he couldn't feel it.

He still hated me, I could see it all over him. I still hated him, my eyes must have told him right back. "You don't have a clue what you're fucking talking about," he told me. "Plenty of people have done things with me because they want to."

I stared straight at him. "Who? Tell me."

My heart was racing, preparing myself for the end, but the end didn't come. His eyes were fierce as he propped himself against the counter, wrapping his hand up in a fresh towel. "Right from the beginning people have done things with me because they want to," he said, and then he told me.

Lucian Morelli stood against his kitchen counter, and he told me about Bethany Fryers, the very first girl he punished and how she cried out for him in pleasure as well as in pain. It gave me tingles where it shouldn't, and my heart was still racing as fast at his descriptions, and that was about more than what he did to her. It was about the dirty sparkle in his eyes as he relived the memories.

He'd had feelings for Bethany Fryers.

Even if he didn't want to admit feelings for anyone or anything in this world, Lucian Morelli once had feelings for Bethany Fryers.

I found myself wondering what she looked like, and what she sounded like and just what it was about her that drove him so wild. Because she did. She drove him wild. Beneath his evil walls, and his callous ways, and his not giving a shit for anyone, that woman drove him wild.

"There you go," he told me when he'd finished recounting her story. "She fucking wanted it."

I had flutters when I spoke next. "So if you liked her wanting it so much, why did you stop choosing people who wanted to enjoy it?"

His voice turned to spite. "Because I like power. Because I take whatever I fucking want. It's about my fucking pleasure, I don't give a shit about anyone else's."

"Good for you, Mr. Selfish," I said and knew as soon as the words left my mouth that I'd pushed the attitude too far. He was on me in one of my frantic heartbeats, his bloodied hand tight around my throat, towel cast aside.

I felt his blood on me, still hot. It gave me chills, picturing how it would be my blood feeling like that if he chose to cut me. "I like power," he said. "Remember that."

He forced my thighs apart enough to press himself against me, and even in my choked state I found I was moving against him.

I wanted to be Bethany Fryers. *I* wanted to be the little blonde girl who drove him wild.

His eyes were evil, but there was depth in them, a curiosity that danced with mine.

"You look like her, you know," he told me, and it gave me a whole new wave of shivers. "At that masked fucking ball, you looked like her. I should've known you were fucking trouble then."

I tried to speak, but his choke hold wouldn't let me. He freed me enough to take in breath, and I sucked in a decent lungful before I found my voice. "You didn't realize it, did you?" I asked. "You hadn't thought about me looking like that girl, not until tonight. I can see it."

"Fuck you," he said. "You can't see shit about me."

But he was wrong. I could. I was getting to know him and his monster ways, even if he didn't want me to. Just as he was getting to know me and my crazy ways right back.

I was still moving against him when he spoke next, still desperate as he pressed his mouth to my ear.

"Now then," he whispered. "Seeing as you know some of my filthy secrets, it's time you told me some of yours."

Chapter Eighteen

Lucian

I FELT LIKE someone had scraped my insides out and laid them on a platter on the counter. I'd never felt like it before. Exposed, like parts of me had been spewed from my center.

The realization that Elaine had reminded me of Bethany Fryers from the very first sight of her at Tinsley Constantine's masked ball was a hammer. Was that where the fixation had come from? Or did I simply have a type, regardless of the trauma surrounding these women.

The curve of her pretty little chin. The slope of her neck. The blonde waves cascading from her, and those pretty blue eyes. Yes, she reminded me of Bethany. They were both beautiful young women. But they were also drastically different.

Were the comparisons between them simply happenstance?

Was I trying to atone for past sins?

I'd done my best to blank out my early memories of Bethany. Somehow, I knew she was a weakness in my perfect strength. I'd long since lost track of the girl who'd first captivated my fetishes, and I'd wanted to. I didn't want even a hint of her in my life.

I was uncomfortable with the swing of the balance—her knowing more about my past than I knew about hers. I didn't tolerate any form of weakness in myself, and that's what it felt like.

I felt weak. It made my words lash out at her as they came. "I'm serious, Elaine. It's time for you to reveal your dirty secrets. I want to know every filthy little part of you."

She shifted on her feet, nervous. Still, she couldn't hide that addictive curiosity in her stare. "I don't have to tell you anything, Lucian," she said, but again there was no venom in it. She couldn't have mustered any if she'd tried. I could smell her temptation to talk to me. It was ripe in her shallow little breaths. She wanted to share.

"You owe me your fucking life," I said, knowing cruelty would compel her more than kindness. "The Power brothers would have killed you by now if I hadn't taken you."

"I don't give a fuck," she said, but again, there

was no venom in it.

The standoff arced between us, laced with a concoction I didn't understand. Hate, disgust, retribution, want, *need*. I hated needing anything. Need was something I could usually snuff out with a click of my fingers, getting whatever I wanted in a flash, but not with her. Not with Elaine.

"You'd better start using that tongue of yours," I said to her, "or I really will make you pay back the debt. I'll make you pay in ways so vile, you could never imagine."

She raised her chin at me, proud, even though she was a wreck, standing in my kitchen, with crusty bloodied thighs, swamped in my shirt. "You would get off on my secrets," she told me. "You'd do nothing but laugh in my face. You'd like them."

I would've usually agreed with her. Her stories should give me nothing but inspiration for how I wanted to make her suffer in my grip, but I wasn't feeling it. The twist in my gut was another one of those crazy sensations that made me want to retch. Feelings? Emotional pain? *What they did to me,* she said. Who hurt you, little doll? The thought made me clench with rage.

"Who did things to you?" I asked her, and her

chin dropped, eyes on the floor.

"It's none of your business," she said, her impudence nowhere to be seen. "I'm not having you laugh at me like that. Fuck me up all you want, but I'm not having it."

I stepped closer and tipped her face up to mine. "You know I've got congenital insensitivity to pain. You know things that nobody else on this planet knows about me. You'd better start talking to fix the imbalance. Secrets or pain, Elaine. Your fucking choice, but make it now."

Her eyes were so sad when they met mine. "Yeah, well at least I get a choice for once in my life. I didn't think it would be Lucian damn Morelli who'd be giving me one."

My stare was solid on hers. "Who hurt you, little doll?"

She took a breath and the strength in her shoulders collapsed, leaving her just a tiny slip of a creature against the counter. Her fight was leaving her in the most beautiful of ways. Her butterfly wings were deathly still as she gave up her flickering attempts to fly away.

She was calm in a way that surprised me, and it was strangely attractive.

A sigh. "Seriously, Lucian. I don't want you laughing at me."

"I'm waiting."

My gaze was firm. Her resolve was breaking. Those butterfly wings parted for me, just wide enough for me to see that the caterpillar between them was an innocent little baby of a bug who'd never been seen before.

Nobody had seen Elaine Constantine before. Not the real, true broken core of her beauty.

"It's a long story," she told me and I didn't doubt it. "It's a long fucked-up story that's never been told. I tried, when I was young enough to think my words actually meant something to the people around me, only to be called a liar."

I was disgusted by the way her words meant *something* to *me*.

"I believe you," I said.

Chapter Nineteen
Elaine

O F ALL THE people in my life I could have told my secrets to, I would've never believed for a second it would be one of the Morellis. If you'd have asked me to put money on the *least* likely person I would've ever told my secrets to, Lucian Morelli would have been pretty high on the list.

He was my enemy. He was a monster. *My monster.*

I should never have been standing there in his gleaming kitchen contemplating telling him my story, not even one tiny little part of it. I hated myself for even thinking about it.

My mind was spinning through the memories, and my stomach was in knots, physically painful without the haze of drink and drugs to blot them out. I didn't want to relive them. I'd spent almost every waking moment of my life trying to run away, trying to bury it all underneath my bullshit world of escaping. I wanted to escape, at any cost—even if that meant losing my life.

So why the fuck was I about to spill my soul to my nemesis and live those memories all over again?

Holy hell, those memories came roaring when they called as I began to tell my story.

I'd long lost track of exactly when my hellhole of an existence sprang from the picture perfect life I had been living. I had everything that a child should love. Toys and games and clothes, green fields and palomino ponies and brothers and sisters bickering all around me.

Dad was way too busy with Halcyon to give me all that much of his time. He'd see us at dinnertime, but it was barely more than a snippet of family life. And I had to share it with my brothers and sisters. I spent much more time around nannies and teachers than him.

Mom was rigid with her expectations. She told me I could never behave.

I guess it was natural for her to agree with Uncle Lionel when he first suggested I have tutoring. Religious tutoring, he said. There's no one better than Reverend Lynch, he said.

Uncle Lionel dropped me off outside the manor church in the rain one day, leaving me staring up at the towers on the driveway. It was Margaret, his maid, who came outside to collect me. She was as stern as the rest of the people I'd come to know—taking hold of my hand and rushing me inside like I was already due a punishment.

The hallways were filled with huge sprawling paintings of our Lord and Savior, Jesus Christ. I felt tiny and inferior as she marched me upstairs to my dorm room at the end of the corridor. The door was huge and made of oak, it made a deep, dark creak as she opened it.

"This is where you'll be staying," she said, her voice shrill.

My bed was a tiny single with a wrought iron headboard and footboard. There was a bedside table with a plain white lamp, and a tapestry on the wall over it. *The Lord's purpose will prevail.* I found myself wondering what the Lord's purpose would be for me in this place.

They left me alone until dinnertime.

Margaret came for me. She led the way downstairs to the dining hall, and I expected there to be many other girls like me there, but there only two.

Neither of them looked at me.

I sat in the seat Margaret pointed me to, feeling edgy and scared. The other girls leaped to their feet and bowed their heads as a man joined us at the head of the table. I jumped up to join them, not quite sure what I was doing.

"You may be seated," he said.

His voice was so firm it gave me shivers. He was an older man—much older than my father. He had gray hair and a beard and small eyes, and had a religious collar on, in a deep, dark burgundy.

He looked strict. Really strict.

I was given soup and ate it slowly, watching the way the other girls were so neat with theirs. I patted my mouth with a napkin and sat up straight in my chair when I was done, and tried to be like them, even though they looked nothing like me. Neither of them looked anything like me, they were both so quiet. So ladylike, as my mother would say.

I guess that's what they wanted me to be like—*ladylike*.

But I wasn't ladylike. I was Elaine.

The other two girls were dismissed and scuttled away after dinner was done, but I was still sitting in my seat. The man at the head of the table cleared his throat and stared at me, and then he spoke. "Hello, Elaine. I'm Reverend Lynch. I'm here to be your teacher and mentor. But most of all, I'm your connection to our Lord."

I found myself nodding, but I was too scared to smile, even a polite smile the way my mother would have wanted. And definitely too scared to speak.

He seemed satisfied by my silence. "You'll most certainly learn to be a good girl here."

I didn't want to spend another minute in that place. The very last thing I wanted was to be like the other two girls.

Reverend Lynch held out his hand to me, and he had a big golden ring on one of his fingers. "Kiss me," he said, and I felt weird doing it. I didn't usually kiss people's hands.

His fingers were thick and warm. I didn't like the way they felt against my lips, so I pulled away as quickly as I could. I felt strangely icky as he kept his eyes on me, like he was soaking into me somehow. It made the hairs on the back of my neck stand up.

"You're excused now," he told me, and I mumbled *thanks*.

He called Margaret in, and she led me back upstairs. I tried to ask her questions, like who the other girls were and who else would be staying with us, and where I could go in the building outside of my room.

"You'll go wherever you're told," she said, and I didn't ask her again, just headed back to my room and sat on the edge of my bed.

She clasped her hands behind her back as she spoke.

"There are rules," she told me. "You only speak when you are spoken to, and you do whatever you are told. And you must always try your very best in your lessons."

I nodded, but I didn't take it seriously. Grown ups always said stuff like that.

"Good night, Elaine," she said, and I heard the key click in the lock as she left.

I was locked in.

I tried the door handle, but it didn't open. I banged on the door, but nobody came.

I'd never been locked in anywhere, and I was already scared of a night alone with no way out.

There was a nightgown in the wardrobe, but I didn't want to wear it. There was a glass of water on the bedside table, but I didn't want to drink it. I wanted to go home, to my own bed in my own room. I thought it was a nightmare as I stared up at the ceiling that night and tried to sleep in that bed. I was nearly crying like a little baby as I thought about more nights in here, and how Uncle Lionel had promised that I would learn so much. I didn't want to learn. I wanted to go home.

I fell into an uneasy sleep. I was still exhausted when Margaret came through the door the next morning and swore at me for not putting on the nightgown.

I ate oatmeal for breakfast and tried to tell myself it was only one night, and I'm sure it would get a bit easier—meeting some other girls and not being so locked up when they knew I could behave enough not to run away.

I thought the first night was a nightmare. I thought it couldn't get worse.

I was wrong.

CHAPTER TWENTY

Lucian

I'D NEVER HEARD of Reverend Lynch, but he made my hackles rise as soon as Elaine spoke his name. Her stance shifted, scared even after all these years.

"He touched you, didn't he?"

She looked away from me as she answered with a nod of her head. It took her a few long seconds to speak again. "First, it was punishment. I had to write lines out for him in my best handwriting. He let the other girls leave when they were done, but he made me stay, saying I hadn't done well enough." She took a breath before she continued. "I was writing them until late, until I was falling asleep in my chair. That's when he came up behind me."

My heart was pounding as I waited for her to continue, and not in a good way.

Her voice was so gentle as she carried on talking. "He tore up the pages."

"He spanked you, didn't he?"

She nodded, and her cheeks were pinking up. "Yeah, he spanked me. He lifted my skirt up and spanked me over my panties. I was so embarrassed. Humiliated, really—tears streaming down my face. I begged him to stop but he told me to shut up. I didn't know priests used words like that. *Shut up.* It was the worst word I knew at the time."

I thought I would delight in her misery. Maybe that sounds fucked up, but when you've lived a life of jaded hedonism as long as I have, you *are* fucked up. I didn't feel delighted. I felt deeply, starkly horrified at her quiet recounting. "And then what happened?"

"He called Margaret back. I tried to tell her that he'd hurt me. I told her I wanted to call my mother, but she wouldn't listen to me. *Reverend Lynch is a good man. A godly man. Spoiled little girls like you have no business making up lies about him.*"

I tipped my head to the side and tried to act nonchalant, but it was hard. I felt anything but calm at her words. My fists clenched at my sides. "How often did he punish you?"

"I was sent there every weekend in the beginning, even though I begged not to go. Uncle Lionel told Mom it was good for me, and I think she was just relieved to have me out of the house."

"Fuck," I said, the word a sharp bark in the air.

"It was strange. Most of the time he was mean. But sometimes…sometimes he would smile at me as if he was proud. Sometimes he'd tell me that I was a good girl. That I was one of God's beautiful angels. He told me those things, and the worst part is, I'd be so glad. I'd be glad that he thought I was a good girl. Even though I hated him."

"He was a fucking predator. He wanted you to feel that way."

"It was a few months in when I first tried to tell my mother what was happening. She said I'd already whined so much about going. She couldn't believe me anymore, because she thought I was just trying to get out of going. She said I was lazy."

I could imagine Caroline Constantine being an absolute cunt. "How long were you going to Reverend Lynch before his punishments got worse than spankings?"

She struggled with speaking, and I could see it

in her eyes. She was shuffling, uncomfortable. It only made me more determined to hear her speak.

I was ready to push her, but I didn't need to. She took another deep breath then carried on talking.

"A long time. So long that I was getting well used to the spankings."

"And then?"

Her pause was profound as that little caterpillar lived through her memories. "He came into my room at night and asked me to thank him. I was already sore from a punishment. He told me to kiss his hand. That's how it started. I had to kiss his hand and tell him thank you."

I wanted to tell her to stop. It made me feel sick to even hear it, but then, she had to do more than listen. She had to live through it. "Elaine."

"Every night I'd watch the bedroom door. Every night I'd pray that it wouldn't open." Her cheeks were pinked up so beautifully I couldn't tear my eyes away from her.

Oh, the little Elaine Constantine kissing that bastard's cock on her knees. I could have slit his throat right there and then, just by laying eyes on the piece of shit. "He was preparing you, you know that? Right from the beginning, he was preparing you."

"I know," she said. "It's easy to see that when you get a bit older. I'm sure other people would have seen that if they'd have believed me."

"Did you try to tell them again?"

"Yeah, I tried to tell them, but every time I did they'd say I was a liar."

"And none of your sisters went to him?"

She shook her head. "No. I was always the naughty one who needed extra lessons. I felt like a bad person. And it made me act like one. If everyone already believed I was a liar, then what was the point of telling the truth? If everyone already believed I was bad, then I would act like it. Parties. Alcohol. Drugs. None of it matters."

"You matter, little doll."

Her eyes were tearful when they next met mine, and it hit me in the gut, just how beautiful and broken my little butterfly truly was.

Chapter Twenty-One

Elaine

I STILL COULDN'T believe I was telling Lucian my past. I felt sick and vulnerable as I stood there, but it wasn't because of the man who had promised to destroy me, it was because of the men who'd already destroyed me. The man before me was doing anything but laughing at me like I thought he would. He looked pissed off on my behalf, which I wouldn't have expected at all.

The sickness was bubbling inside me as I carried on speaking. I lost track of my own train of thought as I let the words flow free. They just came, unbarred in a way they'd never been allowed to be.

Lucian's eyes were so firm on mine as he digested everything I was saying.

I told him about how Reverend Lynch's *kisses* became *sucks*, and about how he'd tell me I was a good girl as I dropped to my knees and gave him what he wanted.

He'd still spank me, harder and harder.

I got so desperate to get away from Reverend Lynch that I tried to sneak out of the place in the middle of the night. That's when he started using my escape antics as an excuse to shackle me to the wrought iron bed frame at night. He'd say it was because I looked like I was planning to be a bad girl. That was when other men started coming at night.

I should've known what was coming, but I tried not to think about that. My behavior was getting worse and worse at home because I was so angry every minute of the day.

Uncle Lionel told Mom that he would start overseeing my education there. He said he owed it to me as my uncle. But he wasn't anything like my uncle when he was in Reverend Lynch's place.

He would be the one to open the door at night when a man stepped inside. I was already used to kissing Reverend Lynch, but not a few different men at once. Sometimes they would punish me. Sometimes they would praise me. Sometimes they would make me pray.

"Your uncle fucking watched this?" Lucian asked me once I took a pause to breathe.

"He shook their hands as they came inside."

"They were paying him," he told me, and I nodded.

"Probably."

"Definitely," he said. "I've heard of some depraved things, but this is fucking sick. And to think the board wanted to confirm *my* character. Meanwhile, there's men like your uncle and this reverend. An underhanded allegiance of filth between men who think they are something noble."

I retched when I thought of the men who'd come to me at night.

I knew their names. I knew their position in the world. I knew just who they were.

Sometimes, I still came into contact with them. Drink and drugs were my very best friends of all time at those parties.

"They didn't fuck you, did they?" he asked me, and I shook my head.

"Not the regular way. They didn't take my virginity, no. I always thought they might, but they didn't. Nobody has ever done that." I give him a small, sad smile. "Not even you."

"Even their allegiance doesn't warrant the risk of taking the virginity of a Constantine girl."

I felt my cheeks burning as I faced up to telling him another bout of truth. "They took me…in other ways."

His eyes narrowed, and his anger wasn't at me. It was a refreshing thing to see. "They fucked your ass."

It was a statement not a question. My fingers twisted in front of me. "It hurt a lot at first."

"They took turns." Another statement.

"They were long nights."

"When did they start fucking you like that?"

"I'd just turned eighteen," I said. "Old enough to consent. Old enough to refuse. But it didn't matter, because they had already conditioned me to accept them."

"Your parents never suspected?"

"They believed my uncle."

I pictured Uncle Lionel's face when I saw him at our house, and the looks he gave me when nobody else was watching. I hated him so bad I wished I could see him die.

"They always believed him about everything. Every little thing that he said I did. Every lie that came from his rotten mouth."

"And what is he like to you now?"

My response was instant. "An evil piece of shit."

He nodded, but didn't speak. He looked like

he was battling with words of his own.

There was a whole load more I wanted to tell him but couldn't; even then I couldn't find the strength to voice it aloud. I couldn't tell him how they confused me by touching me in places that felt good. I couldn't tell him that they'd started rewarding me with alcohol.

I always said thank you to them.

Thank you for hurting me, thank you for hitting me, thank you for making me do what I'm told.

That's when I got so confused that I started hurting myself when I wasn't around them.

Lucian seemed to see where my mind was going, even though he didn't speak to me. He moved in close, looked down at my legs. I flinched when he touched me then ran his fingers over my cuts nice and slowly. A loud breath escaped me. I expected him to slide his fingers between my thighs and make me come, but he didn't.

His hands stayed focused on my legs.

"How about that for my secrets?" I asked him. "I guess we're about even now."

"Bound in secrets much stronger than blood," he said.

I was sure I saw pity in his eyes as he stared

down at me, and I hated it. I hated pity from the monster. "Go on," I whispered. "I guess it's about time you made me suffer now."

He pulled back from me with a puzzled look on his face. "How the fuck does that work, Elaine? You think I'm going to hurt you for telling me that a group of sick fuckers hurt you first?"

I shrugged, because I didn't know. I never knew how these things worked—punishment and rewards, pain and pleasure. I knew he wasn't a nice guy in any sense of the word. I'd heard plenty of stories about just how fucked up he was and all the girls he'd been with. The ones he'd hurt. He liked pain. And I liked receiving pain.

That's when I got the weirdest pang inside me. I didn't want disgusting pity from a Morelli monster, I wanted some form of respect, even at the end of my life, even if he didn't want to show it.

But that wasn't it, was it?

Even now, kidnapped in this gorgeous place with the promise of my demise ahead of me, I still wanted the Morelli monster to want me. "Take it. Take what you want."

That's when he stepped away from me, taking his attention right back to his coffee machine.

His next words were enough to hurt me, in a way that was alien to any kind of physical pain.

He wasn't looking at me, just stirring his mug. "Right now, I want nothing at all."

CHAPTER TWENTY-TWO

Lucian

I WAS GETTING used to the bizarre sensation known as feelings.

But even so, refusing to fuck a vulnerable Elaine Constantine was something I'd never have expected in this lifetime. I didn't want to touch her, and I definitely didn't want to hurt her. It was something I was unaccustomed to, not wanting another person's pain at my hands.

Fucking hell, what the fuck was wrong with me?

She looked bizarrely annoyed, shifting around on the spot like I'd just insulted her, even though it was the kindest thing I'd ever done. "Are you for real? You don't want to touch me now?"

"I don't want to touch you now."

She laughed a snooty laugh. "I didn't put you down as that much of a saint, Lucian."

"A saint? Hardly." I pulled another mug down and made her a fucking coffee. Her eyes were still burning as she took it from me with a *thanks*.

The strange, perverted fellowship should mean nothing to me. They were just a depraved group of rich pricks. Evil? Yes. But there was plenty of evil in the world.

Elaine Constantine would have been a particularly attractive prospect to men like them. Lionel had been risking his life beyond any kind of rationale to even entertain her involvement with Reverend Lynch and his hellhole.

I hadn't come across that sick fucker, but I was already thinking about who in our extended circle played his game. I knew some of the aristocrats and their secret handshakes. Their names were on the tip of my tongue, but she let out a sigh before I spoke.

"I ran away from home once, when I didn't think I could handle it anymore. I ended up running through this trailer park. I met a boy who was running away too."

"Both of you having picture perfect childhoods, I'm sure."

"He had a black eye. His stepdad was belting him every time his mom wasn't there. Not that she'd have stopped him if she was."

"Very different sides of the spectrum from each other. One rich, one poor. You came from different stratospheres but still ended up in the same situation."

"Rich people like to hurt kids, too. We didn't actually talk about our families much, just walked together, finding some kind of weird friendship in our hell."

I could imagine it as she told me. Two fucked-up teenagers finding solace in each other's company. "You went home, though? You must have."

"Sun came up, and we were freezing cold. I couldn't imagine life outside Bishop's Landing. He went back to his trailer, to the belt and his stepdad. I went back to the Constantine compound, where the cops had been called. My feet were bloody, but all my parents could do was yell at me. They called a child psychiatrist who told them I was a lost cause."

"And that's how you met Tristan."

"We tried to blank out our misery, you know? Tried to find something different from all the shit we were used to, even if we didn't share the details."

"Weren't you tempted to move away?"

She let out a sigh. "Yeah, but Tristan's mom

was sick, and I had everyone around me, and we didn't know where the fuck we would go. We always meant to. We always planned it. When I was almost nineteen Reverend Lynch's school stopped for me, though, and I managed to get Tristan some money for a place of his own."

Nineteen years old. I finished my coffee and put the mug down. "When did you get involved with the Power brothers?"

She sipped her coffee. "A couple years ago. I needed coke."

"When did you get into debt with them?"

"When I ran into them and there was a kid like Tristan there, begging them to give him more time for his debts. I didn't hold off for a second, just said I would pay them for him and got them to let him leave."

Elaine really was naive. I knew exactly what the Powers would have been doing after that point. They'd have made sure she knew about every fuck-up coming to them, knowing full well she'd bail them out with Constantine cash—even when that Constantine cash stopped coming. Her mother would have dried it up like a fucking desert when she'd seen what was happening.

"You kept on doing it, didn't you? Giving cash for the addicts, even when you didn't have any. You racked up debt. It was like suicide by cop, except you wanted suicide by loanshark."

She shrugged. "Not that it matters now. At least then a whole load of people go free."

"They're going to war, you know," I told her. "Your family and the Power brothers are edging up closer on the battlefield."

She scowled at me. "Yeah, well more fool me for giving your family a shot at coming out on top of the whole thing. Not that they will. Your family has nothing on mine."

"Fuck off," I said. "My family has everything on yours."

"Better than being a bunch of assholes."

"Your own fucking uncle sold you out to the sickos."

That shut her up, and she wasn't happy about it. She put her drink down on the counter and tore her gaze away from me, finding the impudence in her gritted jaw all over again.

Even after the secret sharing we still hated each other.

You could never deny it, just how ingrained our loathing for each other really was. My family hated hers and hers hated mine. There was so much crossfire and so much instinct brewing over such a long time that it wasn't even obvious anymore just why or how I hated the woman in front of me as much as I did. I just did. I hated her.

She hated me just as much. I could see it in her folded arms and her scowl.

Fuck it. She could have a fucking night of peace for once in her pathetic excuse for a life.

"You can put the pasta on tonight," I told her. "Let's see just how competent you Constantines are at basic life skills, shall we? Let's see if you can boil water."

CHAPTER TWENTY-THREE

Elaine

I DIDN'T THINK he could possibly be serious, but he was. Even with that raging scowl on his face, he grabbed the packet of pasta from the cupboard and threw it over at me.

I managed to catch it. "You want me to make dinner?"

He pulled a face. "No, I thought I'd throw you a packet of pasta for the hell of it."

"*No, I thought I'd throw you a packet of pasta for the hell of it.*" I almost poked my tongue out, almost. I'm sure he almost gave me some punishment for my attitude, almost. He didn't though. He pulled out a load of cheese and other stuff from the fridge and dropped it on the counter.

"Show me what you can do, little doll," he said, his tone sarcastic.

I had an undeniable urge to show him just how capable I really was. I could make damn pasta. "Do you like spices?" I asked him.

"Is that what you do, is it? Spicy pasta?"

I grabbed the pan from the drawer. "Yeah, I like spices."

"So do I," he said.

I chalked it up as one other crazy little thing I had in common with the monster. I only hoped I remembered just what spices to use. I hadn't cooked in a long time.

He opened one of the cupboard doors up high and pointed the spice rack out to me. I pulled out the paprika and the oregano and the chili pepper. And the cayenne powder.

"The Power brothers want my family to team up with theirs," he said to me, and it hardly surprised me, even though it gave me a fresh surge of resentment.

"Yeah, well. Two sets of assholes together."

His gaze was piercing from across the kitchen, his stance more casual than normal as he slouched back against the counter with folded arms. "Why do you hold on so tightly to the fact that your family are somehow the good guys? You must know they're just as bad."

I did know that, but I hadn't seen it. Not

really. I still held my dad up as some kind of idol in both the media spotlight and our personal life. He was always so steadfast and so strong and managed our empire so perfectly. Or so I believed.

"We're definitely the good guys compared to you," I said. "I've heard plenty of stories about your family and how bad you are."

"Ditto," he told me. "I've heard plenty of stories about yours, too."

I put the pasta in the pan and began to stir. I knew we were both churning and festering with a whole mess of stuff between us. Shared secrets, and rage, and hate, and this weird new sense of casual somehow. It was fucked up, just like we were. We were two peas of fucked-up in a very fucked-up pod.

I was still trying to digest the secrets. I couldn't help but wonder what the hell it must be like in Lucian Morelli's body without even a vague idea of pain. He must be so curious about it. I would be—little miss curious. I was already curious enough about how curious he must be, let alone be that curious for myself.

I wondered if he was wondering what my wreck of a past was like. Maybe he was curious too. Maybe he was wondering the things I had wondered, like just why Uncle Lionel was so cruel to his own flesh and blood.

As it turns out, he *was* wondering that. His next question was right on the mark. "Did your father never suspect your uncle was an utter piece of shit?"

"No," I said, pure and simple. "He wasn't really that involved with Uncle Lionel. Mom and Uncle Lionel had quite a close relationship. I guess she assured Dad that I really did need the lessons and Uncle Lionel really was telling the truth."

"Your uncle is a vile piece of fucking shit," Lucian said, and it took me aback. He actually insulted someone for hurting me. I thought he'd be singing their praises.

"They're still close, Mom and Lionel," I told him. "It's not like I could ever have another attempt at telling her what really happened now that I'm older. She's ashamed to call me her daughter."

I would have usually expected him to laugh and say it's not surprising she would be ashamed of me, considering I was Elaine the fuck-up, but it turned out that expectation of mine was instinct and nothing else. He didn't laugh or say a word like that, just kept on watching me from the other side of the kitchen.

I sighed before I spoke again. "The reason my family are after the Power brothers likely doesn't have anything to do with me, you know? It's probably just from embarrassment and distaste at the Powers thinking they could kidnap one of us."

"The Power brothers would have been crazy to think about striking at your family. They aren't strong enough. That's why they want us to join up with them."

I didn't like the nasty flutter I got at that. I didn't like the thought of the Morellis and the Powers hurting the people I loved. I did love a lot of them. I loved some members of my family enough that I'd be absolutely devastated in grief if anything happened to them—even if my emotions were usually too fucked up by hate to register shit about love.

"Do you think you'll team up with them?" I asked him.

His eyes were cold. "None of your business."

"Yeah, yeah," I scoffed and moved over to the cutting board. "None of my business, whatever. We've shared plenty that's none of each other's business this evening, don't you think?"

He cursed under his breath at me, and I suspected it would be at my chatter, but no. "You're not slicing that fucking salami right, it's too thick to cook properly."

Even through the hatred and the confusion of what the hell was truly going on between us, I couldn't help but smile. "Alright then, Chef Morelli. Why don't you show me just how it's done?"

He didn't reply, just took the knife off me and got to work.

I watched his hands moving so firmly. His fingers so strong.

I watched him.

His stance, his height, his power.

His beauty. Because he was beautiful.

Lucian Morelli was beautiful enough to take my breath away, no matter how many times I truly looked at him like that. "Look at the salami and learn your damn lesson," he told me, and I laughed out loud.

"That's one damn lesson I never thought I'd be having," I said. "I'll take that over the ones from my past any day, thanks."

CHAPTER TWENTY-FOUR

Lucian

PASTA CAME QUICKLY. We headed to the dining table, looking surprisingly like two regular people enjoying their dinner. It was probably the closest I'd ever been to a regular person enjoying their dinner—especially with a little doll to enjoy it with.

I told myself I didn't like it. I watched Elaine picking at her food and told myself that I was going to take pleasure in wrecking her, but it was bullshit.

My mind was all on the sick fucks who'd messed with her.

No matter how hard I tried, I couldn't shake off the rage in me. I wanted to take them down. I wanted to look Lionel Constantine in his lecherous eyes and tell him I was there for his niece and then stab him in the gut and twist the blade.

It would be an action that could only be by my own hand. I could never get Alto involved in that, not now that he was a snake to my father. There's no way I could get the cleanup team involved either; it would never stay silent. Which only left me.

My plan and my outcome. I'd be a fool for even considering it, so why was I planning on checking out the calendar for Constantine engagements? I had no fucking idea.

Elaine made casual conversation with me as we ate. I should have told her to shut her mouth and ignored her completely, but I didn't. She was filled with questions about my life in Bishop's Landing and what my life was like as a boy, through to what damn TV shows I liked.

"I don't have time for TV. Never have."

"Is that all you do?" she asked me. "Work constantly?"

"Work and fuck women."

"Great. Clearly that relaxes you."

It was the sass in her smile that I found so damn impossible to raise my hackles to. I was becoming used to her impudence, seeing it for the shield it truly was. I couldn't help but wonder what woman she would have become if it wasn't for the pieces of shit who'd spent years using her for their sick thrills. If she'd managed to take all that and still made it to this much of a vibrant version of Elaine, then who the fuck would she have been if she'd been allowed to grow in her own sunny garden without the sick fuck gardeners?

Still, that wasn't my consideration and should never even enter my brain space. Elaine was my enemy. My enemy. She'd always be my enemy.

I cut through her bullshit small talk with a fresh question. "Who else did that shit to you?"

She was visibly shocked by my outburst. "Why does it matter?"

My scowl was instant. "Who gives a shit about why it matters? Just open your mouth and give me an answer."

It seems she was becoming used to my ways too. She didn't scowl or frown at my tone. "You must know who it was, Lucian. You know who's in the *fellowship*. You said so."

"Tell me then," I said to her. "Just fucking say it."

She picked at the last of her pasta then put her fork down. "Baron Rawlings," she said. "He was one of them."

I pictured the old man, parading his status.

"Who else?"

She started picking at her pasta again. "Lord Eddington."

I knew it. Eddington was a snide piece of shit. "Keep going."

It took her a minute, and I let her have one, chewing over her answer until she was ready to spit it out. "Colonel Hardwick," she whispered, and I knew why it had taken her a while. Colonel Hardwick was particularly close to her family.

I knew those socialite pricks were regular attendees at social engagements throughout the year. Lord Eddington and Baron Rawlings were from across the Atlantic, but visited often. I imagined they would use Reverend Lynch's place as a stop-off point along with their bullshit social stays.

I also knew that Colonel Hardwick lived out on a rural estate past Bishop's Landing.

Elaine laughed one of her sassy laughs at me as I pondered.

"What are you going to do, Lucian?" she asked. "Hurt them for me?"

I should have laughed right back at her. I tried. I managed a pathetic smirk and little else. I shouldn't kill these bastards. Especially not as retribution for a Constantine.

Fuck knows why I headed to the bathroom once I'd finished my pasta and called up the Bishop's Landing social event scene on my phone. Fuck knows why I looked up the charity presence of them over the next few fundraising events. I checked out the attendee list.

Lord Eddington was at the next one, in just a few days.

I was still brewing on it as I stepped back into the living room and found Elaine curled up on the sofa like she was right at home. Fuck knows why I hovered without cursing her for her ease, then sat down opposite her in the battered old armchair. I didn't have the energy to do anything else. For once in my life my legs were tired, and my brain was tired to match. I had a whole load of spinning thoughts and deadlines and sensibilities I should be focused on—not on who started fucking Elaine Constantine in the ass when she was legal enough to technically invite them to. That's what they'd been doing, of course. Coercing her to the point it would have been *consensual,* and she'd believe it so.

"Are you not heading back into the city, then?" she asked me, her voice tired.

"I will be."

She shrugged. "It's quite a way, back and

forth every day. Aren't you at least going to take some thrill out of being here? I'll bare my ass for you, if you like."

I shook my head at her. "Is that how you flirt?"

She rolled her eyes at me. "You're Lucian Morelli. Lucian Morelli doesn't need offers. Lucian Morelli takes whatever the fuck he wants. And you want my ass again, right?"

I wanted nothing more than my bed upstairs. Fuck heading back into New York City; it would have to wait until morning. I looked at the clock and it was already far later than I'd imagined. The Elaine effect, no doubt, turning the minutes into hours with her chatter. "Get up to bed," I told her, and gestured to the doorway. "Fuck off and take your snarky mouth with you."

She hovered in her seat. I stared at her from across the room.

"I mean it," I said. "Don't hang around until I change my mind. My temper is fucking short."

I guess she came to her senses. She was up like a shot and straight on past me, only stopping to turn around in the doorway and fix me with those pretty blue eyes. "Thanks," she said, and walked away.

I didn't know quite what the fuck she was

thanking me for, but it didn't matter. The way my stomach did a lurch at her smile was all I needed to know.

Elaine Constantine was no fucking good for me. I should stay the damn hell away from her and drive back into New York City where I belonged.

Fuck knows why I climbed the stairs anyway.

Chapter Twenty-Five

Elaine

I HEARD LUCIAN walk past my room on the way to his.

I heard the way he paused outside mine.

My heart raced like a train—two conflicting emotions at once. On one hand the instinctive fear of having a man outside my room was enough to make me feel sick and pull the covers up higher, and on the other...on the other...

I shouldn't even face it. There's no way I should be feeling what was on the other.

He continued on, and a fresh wave of goddamn *something* bloomed up in me.

Hurt. Rejection. Who knows.

One thing I did know was that I wanted Lucian Morelli to want me. I couldn't lie about that to myself anymore. No matter how many times I tried to deny it. I wanted Lucian Morelli to want me. I *needed* Lucian Morelli to want me.

I heard his door close at the end of the landing, and I felt so alone that I pulled the covers up over my head. I knew it would happen. It had to. I'd been revisiting memories I'd been running away from for years. I had no cocaine or alcohol to block it out, and that began to take its toll on me. I felt sick and desperate for the substances I relied on…and more …I felt sick for more than that. I *needed* more than that. God help me, I needed more than that.

Life inside here was messing me up in ways I'd never known. I wasn't even thinking about life outside anymore. I wasn't thinking about the inter-family conflict that was brewing because of me, or how frantic people like Tristan and Harriet would be to bring me back. There were a few of them at least. I hadn't thought about the news reports that might be running on the TV or how Lucian was keeping me away from them this evening. Who knows what they'd be saying now?

Beyond all that, I was torn between thinking about the monsters from my past and the monster down the hall. There it was in the balance—monsters from my past, or the monster down the hall…

I chose the monster down the hall.

I'd spent years believing that touching myself where it felt good was a bad thing, but I couldn't stop my fingers slipping down between my legs as I thought about Lucian. I was thinking about the ferocity in his eyes, and how strong he'd been in the kitchen, and how angry he'd looked as I told him about the men who'd fucked me up. I was thinking about the curse in his tone, and how powerful that was, and how his fingers were so firm as he sliced the salami.

I was thinking about simple things mixed with his beastly soul.

If he even had a soul. He was a Morelli, after all.

I shouldn't have touched myself and thought about him, but I couldn't stop. I thought right back to Tinsley's masked ball where he'd first laid his hands on me and just how much that had swept me away. I thought back to the fear I'd felt in Jemma's apartment when he'd cornered me there, and just how different I was feeling now to the drugged-up mess who'd wanted to die at his hands—because that was the other thing that was changing…I wasn't so sure I wanted to die anymore. For real, I wasn't sure if I wanted to die.

My fingers were fast and light between my legs, teasing me as my breaths quickened. The memories blurred and grew more intense, until I was back next to Stephen Cannon's body with Lucian on top of me, taking my ass. I shouldn't be thinking about that. I shouldn't be thinking about how Lucian had stabbed a man to death who'd been trying to rape me. Because that's what he'd done. My enemy had saved me. Oh fuck, Lucian Morelli had saved me...

My fingers pressed harder to my clit, faster, faster. My breaths were hitching, needy. *Lucian.* My fingers danced, desperate, and my thoughts were tumbling, more and more. More of the monster. More of his hate and his spite.

More of what he could do to me...because I wanted it.

I couldn't help but want it. I wanted him to be rough with me, and control me, and show me his strength and his power. I wanted him to be the first one to fuck my pussy and make me truly his. I wanted him to make me truly his.

Holy fuck, I wanted Lucian Morelli to truly make me his.

And then I wanted to stay that way.

I wanted to belong to Lucian Morelli.

Please no. Please.

My fingers were circling hard enough that I held my breath and raised my hips from the bed. I tried to slow my breathing but I couldn't, I was too lost in my thrills. My clit was alive and screaming, my body was desperate for the man who was out to tear me apart, and I couldn't stop myself from coming. I couldn't. I couldn't.

I came to the fantasy of belonging to Lucian Morelli for all time.

It was the most bad girl thing I'd ever done. I should never have the fantasy of belonging to Lucian Morelli for all time. He was a Morelli. An enemy I should be out to destroy, just as he was out to destroy me. They'd always been out to ruin our family, and now they might do it. The Morellis might team up with the Power brothers and hurt my family...because of me.

I rolled over in bed and caught my breath, my mind churning.

I had so many questions and fears and guilty thoughts and needs.

This should've been a simple case of kidnapping. I thought I'd be bound up and punished until I was nothing but a broken shell of the woman. How the holy fuck was I eating pasta and talking about hobbies? How was it *me* trying to push him into hurting me? Were we in some kind of surreal dimension where I'd been thumped on the head and woken up in cuckoo land?

Jesus, Lucian had been the one person in my life to hear my story. I'd told him that. I'd told him all my secrets, and he'd listened to them all without so much as a smile at my suffering.

This really was cuckoo land.

I was still lying on my side under the covers when I pulled my knees up to my chest and tried to settle down to some sleep. I needed to stop my whirring mind, but it wouldn't slow down, churning, churning. That's when it started churning over the things I'd told the Morelli heir—all of the nasty nights I'd spent afraid of who was coming and what they were going to do to me. Once again I was back in my own pool of fear, once again craving the drink and drugs to block it out of me. Once again there was no coke and champagne to bail me out.

The night was quiet and cold, what little was left of it. The closed door was an ominous shadow in the corner of the room, and the covers over my head didn't stop me peering out at it, like I'd learned to do so many times in my past. I started shaking, like always. My mouth turned dry, like always. I gripped my knees tighter to my chest, like always.

As always, it didn't work. I was just the broken girl shaking in the dark.

I switched the light on, but it didn't make the slightest difference, just seemed to make the closed door more ominous. It should have been ominous given the beast that was down the hall, and how he may come for me. But it wasn't. The beast down the hall wasn't ominous at all. Strange but true. The beast down the hall felt like my safety, not my fear.

I threw back my covers and swung my feet down onto the floor. I had no idea what the hell I was thinking as I crept my way across the room and pressed my ear to the closed door.

I couldn't hear him out there. He was definitely still in his room. Definitely still down the hall, probably deep in slumber since he undoubtedly had a trip into New York City in the morning…the *early* morning…

My crazy took on a fresh level of insane when I eased the door handle down and peeked my way out onto the landing. It was dark, and empty. Lucian's door was closed at the end, I could just about see it in the shadows.

I held my breath as I stepped out. I still had his damn shirt on, and it felt floaty against my thighs, still sore from where I'd cut them earlier. I ghosted my way closer to his room with my heart pounding and my nerves on fire, and I should've raced back to my shitty bed in the other shitty room, but I didn't. I pressed myself up against his door and placed my hand on the handle.

Please, God, what the fuck am I doing?

I turned the handle as gently as I could, and I was shaking. I was a wreck. I was insane as I slowly opened the door.

I was fully expecting Lucian to sit stark upright in bed, then come charging after me, dragging me back down the hallway and belting me at the very least before locking me back in my room. But no. He didn't.

Lucian Morelli was asleep in his bed, fast asleep to the world.

I should've stolen his keys and got the hell out of there—driving his car back into the city and condemning him for good, but I didn't. Hell knows why, but I didn't.

I waited a full minute at least before I dared to ease the covers back just enough to slip myself inside of them. I stayed right on the edge of the mattress, trying not to disturb him, keeping as far away as I could. Still, I couldn't help myself. His warmth was too inviting. Bizarrely enough, I felt safer next to the monster than I had anywhere else in the whole damn world. Nobody would ever get to me in this place...nobody but the monster himself.

It was sad but fucking true that the monster was fast becoming the one man I *wanted* to get me, only this time it wasn't about him wiping me out and freeing me from my pitiful misery…

This time it was about becoming the monster's prey in a whole other way…

I couldn't deny it…I wanted the monster to love me enough to keep me safe…

It was true…

Oh my God, it was true…

I wanted the monster to love me.

Chapter Twenty-Six

Lucian

I HAD NEVER overslept in my life, not like I did that morning. I awoke from my bed with the daylight fast streaming through the window, cursing myself...only to find Elaine Constantine in my bed next to me.

My little doll was in my bed next to me.

I stared in shock at the figure at my side, curled up tight with her knees to her chest, sleeping as soundly as I had been. My first instinct was to shake her the fuck awake and drag her the fuck out of there, but I didn't. I fucking didn't. I just stared at her like a fucking fool.

Elaine Constantine was in my bed.

In my fucking bed.

Nobody was ever in my bed, let alone a fucking Constantine.

It was when I twisted and reached for my

phone on the bedside table that she stirred beside me. It was when she stretched out her arms, still dressed in my shirt, that I realized just how fast asleep she had been. It appears she was going as damn fucking crazy as I was, choosing to sneak into her soon-to-be destroyer's bed in the middle of the night.

She rolled over, and that's when she tensed and leaped up in bed. She was terrified in that moment, eyes wide as she registered just how hard I was staring at her.

"I, um…" she began. "The room down there was…"

"Was what?" I asked, my voice gruff with sleep.

"It was, um…"

I pointed a finger at her. "We're not having a fucking sleepover, Elaine."

She looked annoyed at that, throwing the covers off and moving to get out of there, but I took hold of her arm before she managed it. "I'm *sorry*, alright?" she said in her usual snarky tone, then tried to wrench away from me, but I wouldn't let her.

I yanked her back around until she was facing me, and I couldn't work out what she was thinking as I met her eyes, still trying to squirm her way from my grip. "You must be insane," I said. "Climbing in bed with me. Absolutely fucking insane."

"Yeah, well, I probably am," she said, and gave up the fight.

She slumped down and let out a sigh, and I found myself staring at her in a whole new way. Brave woman. She had climbed into bed with me. Next to me. Because she wanted to, not because she was dragged there. She really did have some fire in her.

My phone vibrating on the bedside table pulled me back to my senses. Crap. Eleven missed calls from various people at Morelli Holdings...and one of them was my father.

"We'll talk about this when I get back," I growled at her.

"Why don't you drop me off in the city on your way there?"

I scoffed at her. "Like I'm ever going to drop you back in the fucking city, Elaine. I'm not letting you go. Ever. So get that idea out of your head. Nothing's changed because we had a bit of a chat in the kitchen last night."

"And ate some pasta," she added, and there it fucking was again, that cheeky smile. "Don't forget the wonders of slicing salami just right,

Lucian. We're almost besties now."

"Fuck you," I said and pulled my pants on.

I left her cross-legged on my bed, in my damn shirt, with her messy blonde curls, looking like a conquest, even though I'd never had one. Elliot Morelli would make fun of me if he knew.

I didn't say goodbye and neither did she.

Traffic was insane as I made my way into the city, and I tried to play it cool as I returned the calls on my phone. All except my father's. I didn't return the call from my father.

My gut was twisted up as I neared Morelli Holdings. I had no idea what the hell I was going to say to my father when he started asking questions.

As it turned out, I didn't have all that long to think about it.

He was already waiting for me when I arrived.

CHAPTER TWENTY-SEVEN

Elaine

I STAYED IN Lucian's bed for a long while after I heard him disappear. His bed was much more comfortable than the one he'd given me—no surprise there—but it was about more than that. It smelled like him. The covers smelled like my monster. I was engulfed by the scent of him.

I could've stayed there for days like a school-girl with a crush.

I finally dragged myself downstairs when the morning was truly underway, dropping myself onto the sofa and switching on the TV. The news channels blared out about my disappearance. People I'd never met before were being inter-viewed, commenting and speculating on what had happened to me. There was a police helpline to call with any information.

My family was all over the channels with

tearful requests for people to find me. It ate me up inside to think Harriet or Vivian were crying for me.

Part of me expected to see Tristan talking about my disappearance. There was a big chunk of me that thought maybe he would be all guns blazing to let the world know about my interactions with Lucian, but there was nothing. Not a peep from him. I hoped he was doing okay. Just as long as nobody had reached him, or worse, silenced him.

I turned my mind away from that as best as I could.

Lucian wouldn't have needed to silence him because he had nothing to say that would have any real weight to it. I left a note on my counter. I blamed it on the Power brothers in my own handwriting. Tristan would have believed my note. Not that I expected him to believe everything I said, but this was beyond my usual level of lying, for sure.

I got a weird tickle inside me as I pulled myself away from the TV to grab some breakfast. It was a rush of something in my stomach. *Instinct.* I stopped on the spot in the hallway and turned to the front door, and there was something about it, an impulse to check the handle. I reached out and didn't expect to get anywhere, because surely not. I'd heard it slam when Lucian was on his way out, and he'd always lock it, of course he would, only this morning he was rushing.

Maybe…just maybe…

My heart leapt a mile when the door swung open with a creak.

Oh my God, I was free! Free!

It felt so weird stepping onto the porch, because I could run. There were lanes and tracks and roads stretching back out toward the city. No doubt I could find someone, *anyone* to hear my pleas and screams and efforts to get heard. I could have Lucian Morelli condemned before he'd ever make it back out of Morelli Holdings. I could destroy him. I *could*.

I grabbed my discarded shoes from behind the door and slipped them on with shaking hands. The world outside was fresh and cold, and the sun was up bright in the sky. Yeah, I could run from here. The driveway was long, sure, but it was doable. I could wrap up in warm clothes and make my dash for it. I could see the back of Lucian Morelli for all time, and cause an inter-family battle that would stand one hell of a good chance of swinging in the Constantines favor, just so long as I could shake off this damn craziness about wanting him…

I could do it. Surely, I could. I should be able to. I should definitely be able to. He was nothing but an enemy of mine who wanted to see me torn apart, and I needed to remember that. I should damn well remember that with every breath in my body. *Yes.*

Fuck. I cursed myself out loud when I felt the pang of *no* in my belly. *No.* What the fuck was no? But it *was* no. I couldn't do it. Fuck my life, I couldn't. There was no damn way I could shake off the damn craziness about wanting him. Not in a million damn years.

Fuck it.

I wandered around the yard, still hoping to talk some sense into myself. The grounds around the house looked pretty wild, compared to the sleek modernity of the interior. I doubted Lucian was nearly as good a gardener as he was a pasta maker. I couldn't imagine him ever taking active care of the space. I'd never really had a garden, not of my own.

I stepped out onto a patch of grass and spun myself around, truly soaking it all in. There were big sprawling trees and plenty of scope to make this space into something truly amazing. I could do that. I could learn to. I could read some books, and watch some YouTube videos, and get a grip of what would work and where. I cursed myself again as I thought it through. It was nothing but more craziness that would never happen. I needed to stop living such a dream.

I kept the front door open as I made myself some pancakes for breakfast, unable to face shutting the world out. I ventured out onto the lawn with my plate, loving the breeze in my face as I munched my food with a smile. Yeah, I liked it out here. I really damn well liked it.

I didn't want to watch anymore shit TV, not when there was so much better outside to be looking at. I wrapped up warm in one of Lucian's designer sweaters from his wardrobe, then tried to find some gardening equipment in the garage. It surprised me to find a set of spades and trowels ready and waiting. Maybe he did have a tiny streak of gardener in him. Maybe I'd even find out.

I was outside on the nearest flower bed on the lawn, dredging up weeds with a trowel when I finally condemned myself for what I was doing. Surely I couldn't work on Lucian Morelli's countryside garden? But I could. I did.

In one of the most bizarre and surreal choices of all time, I, Elaine Constantine of the Constantine family line, turned her back on escaping from the Morelli monster's mansion and tended to his goddamn garden instead.

Go fucking figure.

Chapter Twenty-Eight

Lucian

NO ONE WANTED to meet my eyes as I walked toward my father in the main lobby of Morelli Holdings. He watched me approach with his usual cold expression. No, they didn't want to look, but they couldn't help it. My father meeting me in the lobby was a fucking spectacle.

He put his hand out at the last second, and I shook it.

"Meeting room." He was a terse motherfucker. "Now."

My father walked beside me to the elevator. It was a silent, tense ride to the ninth floor. He stalked in front of me on the way into the room and took a seat at the head of the table.

I sat across from him, leaned back, and met his eyes.

"You're having a fucking mental breakdown,"

he said.

"Hardly. I've just been busy."

"Busy chasing down the Constantines?"

I pretended that I didn't understand his logic. "Excuse me?"

"Are you finding more Constantines to fuck now that Elaine has been taken?"

"Is that what Alto told you?" I didn't move, other than to release a breath. I wasn't going to let him think he was making me nervous. A strange fucking feeling, being nervous.

He leaned back in his seat to match me. Two Morellis in the same pose, staring at each other across the meeting table. "He heard people are chasing after Tinsley."

A wave of annoyance at Trenton twisted in my gut. I could have killed him right there and then. Still, I should be grateful. The accusation had fuck all of a Morelli criminality to it compared to the true extent of my crimes.

"I didn't come here to discuss Trenton's rumors with you. Is there something you wanted to say? If you don't, I have other things to attend to."

His jaw clenched, face reddening. His irritation was palpable. Something else, too. "You need to come back to Morelli Holdings."

"Or else what?" I was flippant. An asshole. Just like him.

"Or the board will know you'll leave whenever you damn well please."

"Then the board would be right, because that's exactly what I'm doing."

He swore. "Christ, Lucian. You're lucky you can't feel pain. I'd whip you fucking raw."

"If you laid a hand on me, you'd regret it. But I'll make the decision much easier for you. As long as I'm gone, I'm not a threat. If you want me to come back? Make me CEO." I didn't think he'd actually do it, no matter how desperate he was for me to come back. It was more about smoke and mirrors. Let him think that I wanted to be CEO, when what I really wanted was to fuck my Constantine doll. She was only a short ride away.

"You leave the Constantines the fuck alone. We team up with the Power brothers or we do nothing at all. No fucking thing. No digging, no chasing, no attempting to tear them down."

Part of me wanted to laugh in his face and say he had no idea what the hell I'd been doing. Instead I used the opportunity to use my truths as my strengths. "I've had fuck all to do with Tinsley Constantine," I told him. "I can assure you of that."

He paused for long seconds, our eyes fixed firm and cold on each other's. "Good. You'd better keep it that way." He leaned in closer. "What the fuck are you thinking, Lucian? What the hell is going on with you?"

"I've been busy."

"Hanging out in the BDSM club?"

"Something like that."

It struck me in that moment just how distant I'd grown from my family. He was referring to a point in the past where I'd been heavily involved with Violent Delights, happily focused on indulging my thrills with the women there. "Are we done with this little father-son conversation? I've got more important things to be doing than justifying my sexual interests."

I knew there was a whole world of questions in his throat that he wanted to lash out at me, but he didn't. Our lack of closeness had destroyed any bridges into my privacy he'd ever managed to build.

He gestured to the door, as though this was still his kingdom and not mine. I was already up and leaving when he spoke again.

"You go anywhere near any more of the Constantines without Power brothers' approval and

I'll make an example of you. You'll wish you'd never been born."

It was another threat in the same vein, the Constantine vein. The vein that was turning me into the biggest fool I'd ever known. Still, it didn't even touch me.

I smiled. "Are you upset because I'm not obeying your orders? Or because the stock prices for Morelli Holdings are down more than they've been in years?"

"You step up to the plate here at Holdings, or you step down until you can sort your shit out. Play your bullshit games or hang out at your BDSM club, but don't ruin Morelli Holdings."

"I'm not ruining anything. You're doing a great job of that by yourself."

I wasn't interested in what my father was threatening. It didn't even bother me that Morelli Holdings was struggling. Well, it did bother me. Because it harmed more people than just me and my father. It impacted my mother and my sisters. It impacted the board. Our stockholders. And it really impacted the thousands of employees.

So yes, Morelli Holdings mattered to me.

But it was less important than Elaine Constantine.

The truth was a hard one to accept, and it

took my breath away before I made it back to the elevator. I'd never been floored by emotion in my life. I'd never known such a rush of conflict, never mind how to fucking deal with it.

I forced myself into the elevator and selected the lobby. It was the slowest descent of my life.

I couldn't walk the line between Morelli Holdings and Elaine. There was no way I could juggle the two of them. I couldn't indulge the temptress and my wants for her and still wrestle control away from my father. It was impossible. The whole thing was fucking impossible.

I had to make my choice.

It should have been Holdings. Of course, it should've been Morelli Holdings.

I could take that sweet virginity of hers and revel in her pain and dismiss her into the trash where she belonged as a Constantine. Only it wasn't Holdings I wanted.

It was her.

CHAPTER TWENTY-NINE

Elaine

WHEN LUCIAN'S CAR pulled up in the driveway, I was still outside with a trowel in the flower bed. My heart leaped as I realized just what the hell I'd done by staying in this place and risking my life every second I was around him, but it was too late.

My decision had already been made.

The sun was still high in the sky, the afternoon barely half done when he'd parked up in the garage and was heading to the front door with his keys in his hand. I could have hidden in the bushes and pretended I'd already run away from him, but I didn't.

"Over here, honey!" I waved my trowel in the air.

The monster stopped and stared, fixing me in his piercing eyes as he stomped in my direction. I carried on digging the soil and pulling the weeds out, like it wasn't the most insane decision I'd ever made and I wasn't kidnapped in a hole of a place belonging to my archenemy.

"What the hell are you doing? Are you out of your fucking mind?"

His tone was blunt, but it wasn't aggressive. His eyes were wild but not full of hate as he stared down at me.

I shrugged. "Does that surprise you?"

He couldn't hold back a smirk. "You're doing alright on that. I would've expected a lot more wallowing and begging on the coke front."

Yeah, I would too. I'd surprised myself there. I was firmly on the same page as him on expecting the wallowing and begging for lines of powder. That and bottles of fizz.

Lucian tossed his keys in his hand as he scoped out the pile of weeds I'd been digging up. I did a silly little bow from my knees and waved the trowel in the air like some kind of superstar as I spoke again.

"Yes, I know, I know. It seems I am quite the capable gardener, doesn't it? Despite me not being a success with slicing salami."

He tried to scowl. "There's you with that sassy mouth again. You should be a more convincing kidnap victim, you know. Maybe then I'd take pity on you and let you go."

I found my bitchy tone at that. "Screw you and your pity. I'll never bathe in pity, no matter how rough it gets. I'm no *pet* for anyone. Not outside of the bedroom anyway."

We were both staring at each other, and the Morelli-Constantine hate should have been bristling as strongly as ever. He should have been dragging me inside and telling me I'd missed my escape chances and more fool me, and I should be cursing myself for ever considering staying in this damn place, but we weren't doing any of it, just damn well staring.

"I left the door unlocked, I'm guessing?" he asked me. "That's what happens when you sneak into my bed overnight and fuck my alarm over. Maybe you should try it more often."

"I didn't fuck your alarm over. You were sleeping so deep you didn't get up in time."

"Regardless. I rushed out and left the door unlocked, did I?"

I shrugged like it was no big deal. "I noticed it on my way to get some breakfast. I've had plenty of time to get the hell away from here."

"Yes," he said. "You have. So why didn't you?"

I didn't really have an answer for that. Not one that made sense. I couldn't tell him that the thought of leaving him and this place gave me a sick pang in my stomach and nothing but a sense of dread at walking away. I could hardly say that I'd stayed wrapped up in his bed covers for hours after he'd gone this morning, just to smell him. I couldn't admit that I'd fantasized about making this place into a dream home that I could dance around for the rest of my life.

"Really, Elaine," he pushed. "Why didn't you run?"

We stared at each other some more, and I couldn't fight the flutters in my belly. Something was happening between us...even under the hate and the craziness and the utter carnage in our world, something was happening...

"I don't know," I lied, then realized I had a question of my own. "Why are you back so soon? You can't have been in the city more than a couple of hours."

"You're asking for it, you know that?"

"I'm asking you to fuck me, you know that? Even if it's in the grass here, just get your cock out and fuck me, please."

We stared again, and my mind was churning, thinking. Why the hell was Lucian Morelli in a garden in the middle of nowhere while his empire was moving at full speed in the city? It didn't make any sense. None of this made any sense in the goddamn slightest.

"You are crazy, Elaine. You could have been back anywhere else in Bishop's Landing by now. You could have had me imprisoned. It would have been my mistake for leaving the fucking door unlocked."

"Could have been, but I'm not," I said. "I guess I really am crazy, aren't I? Or maybe you left it open on purpose. Maybe this was a test. Am I passing?"

Lucian Morelli grabbed me up from my knees and slammed me into the wall at the side of his crappy house. I thought he would hurt me, finally…

I thought he would tear me apart, this time for good…

But he didn't. Oh fuck, he didn't.

Lucian Morelli slammed me into the wall at the side of his crappy house and kissed me like he meant it. He kissed me until I moaned into his mouth and kissed him back.

Chapter Thirty

Lucian

I COULDN'T FIGHT it any longer. The truth was too strong in my mind. Elaine was too good a temptress, and I couldn't resist her anymore. I pressed her up tight to the outside wall, and I kissed her, only this time it wasn't laced with hate or spite or the need to tear her to pieces. This time it was about something I'd never felt before, something as alien to me as pain.

I was in love with her.

I was in love with a Constantine.

Both the Constantines and the Morellis would kill me for my crime, and I wouldn't blame them. I'd kill *myself* for my crime if I didn't love myself too damn much.

There was as much truth and need in the way she kissed me back. We were frantic, desperate beyond belief as we made our way along the wall toward the front porch. I backed her in through the front door with my mouth still hungry on hers, and it didn't matter which direction we were headed in, just as long as her body was next to mine. I was confused and split apart by conflicting desires. I wanted to save her from her past and savage her in her future both at once. I craved her pain and her tears and her cries of my name, only this time it wasn't power and punishment driving me, it was more than that. It was fascination for her body and her desires and her needs, because she needed it like I did. Elaine was a masochist to my sadist, the yin to my yang, the light to my dark, the blonde to my black.

Elaine was the Constantine to my Morelli.

She mumbled against my mouth. "Hurt me, Lucian. Make me yours."

I growled and bit her bottom lip, shunting her toward the living room. "You're already mine. Your pussy will be the jewel in my crown."

"It's given, not stolen." Her words gave me another chill of a thrill. She wasn't stolen, she was given. I'd never wanted anything I'd been given before. I'd always claimed or bought it, taking everything on my own terms.

Strangely enough, I didn't want to take the jewel in the crown—not so quickly or frantically.

I wanted to enjoy every second of holding back.

Elaine was wearing so much of my crap against the cold. I tugged my sweater up and over her head and cast it away. I tore my shirt apart so hard the buttons sprang off, and there she was, beautiful in her bra. I tugged my pants off her, oversized and hanging, and she wasn't wearing any panties underneath. She was naked perfection as I unclipped her bra and thrust her through the living room doorway.

I held her wrists over her head against the living room wall, pinning her firmly enough that she let out a moan. She rubbed against me, that sassy smile of hers so pretty it sent me wild. I ground my hips against hers, then forced her legs open with my thigh, and we were right back there, in the bathroom at Tinsley Constantine's ball. If I would've believed in fate, I would've believed in it in that moment. If there was such a thing as destiny this would be ours, star-crossed lovers whose paths belonged as one, no matter how much it would cost them.

"Keep your hands above your head," I growled at her, and she nodded. "Good girl."

My fingers slipped down her throat and along her collarbone. My mouth was back on hers as I took hold of her tits and squeezed hard enough that she moaned against my lips. I squeezed harder, twisted, made her moan louder. My thigh rubbed against her pussy with a force that made her cry out, but still she squirmed against me. Yes, Elaine was a masochist. She wanted this.

I was as desperate as she was as I dropped to my knees before her. I, Lucian Morelli, dropped to my knees in front of a Constantine with the sole desire to pleasure her. The very thought was insanity. My mouth was hungry for her pussy, my tongue was a snake against her clit, around and around in a rhythm that had her hands in my hair.

"No!" I barked. "Hands above your head!"

She did as she was told. Her arms were up straight, hands flat to the wall as I ate her out with renewed vigor. She was mine. Her pussy was mine.

Elaine tensed up as I did the unthinkable and prepared her beautiful slit for my cock. I wet my own fingers before I pushed two inside her, slowly enough that she murmured. I was so gentle. Even as I nipped at her clit, I was gentle inside her.

"My God, Lucian! Please! Yes! More!"

I didn't give her more. I made her wait, slowly, slowly, back and forth.

"Please! More!" she cried.

"Quiet!" I grunted, and once again she did as she was told, holding her breath as I teased her with my tongue.

I was going to make Elaine Constantine come with my fingers inside her. I wanted to hear her come, from my knees, with my mouth on her pussy and my fingers rammed deep.

I worked like a perfect beast against her clit, licking, sucking, nibbling as she whimpered. She tensed and she squirmed as I slid two fingers into her, and her hands dropped down the wall a touch, even though she did what she was told and kept them raised. She moaned and pushed against me, and slowly, ever so slowly, she lost herself to the sensations as I circled my fingers inside her, my tongue lapping at her clit, feeling her tension as the orgasm bloomed inside her. Her pussy was divine, a flower that would be the most beautiful thing in the world to stretch open wide when I thrust my cock inside her. Only it wouldn't be now. I would be holding out on those petals until I couldn't stand it anymore.

The noises were beautiful as she crested. Her murmurs were the most intoxicating sound. My face was wet with her juices when she shuddered and buckled and gasped to find her breath. Elaine Constantine was a perfect little doll when she came for me.

I still tasted her when I got to my feet and pushed my tongue in her mouth to dance with hers.

I tugged hard on her nipples and claimed her hot mouth with mine until she was squirming and fucking drooling.

Fuck, I loved kissing Elaine.

I was in *love* with Elaine fucking Constantine.

She wrapped her arms around my neck and held me close, and I wanted it. I couldn't deny it anymore, not any of it. I wanted Elaine Constantine to hold me. I'd never wanted anyone to hold me in my life, but her touch was magic to me.

I thought she'd be done and finished when I pulled away from her mouth and let go of her nipples, but her breaths were still fast and light, and her eyes were wide on mine.

"Don't stop," she whispered. "Please, Lucian, don't stop."

I thought she wanted my tongue back on her clit, but she didn't. Her cheeks were flushed pink when she dropped her eyes from mine, squirming nervous.

"Please, Lucian. Hurt me some more. I need more pain."

Chapter Thirty-One

Elaine

I WAS STILL flying high when Lucian pushed me forward over the arm of the sofa. My breaths were still shallow and my clit was still tingling as I bared my ass to him and he slapped me, hard. I loved it. The sensations set me alight. *This* was the kind of pain I needed above any other. I needed to be hurting, but high, and I was so high I was soaring…being hurt by the man I loved.

The man I *loved*.

The very thought had me grinning as he hit me.

His slaps were quick, but not so quick they had me squealing. He was paced and steady, and that's when I knew it, for the very first time I'd ever known it. He was hurting me for me and not for him. He was giving me pain for my pleasure and not his own. It was the most amazing feeling.

My flesh was alive, burning just right where he'd hit me. I couldn't hold back a moan as he slipped his fingers between my thighs and pushed them inside me, teasing just like he'd done before. This time I was ready for him. I was bucking back against him for more. More fingers, more slaps, more Lucian. More Lucian, more Lucian, more Lucian.

The gorgeous beast gave me more Lucian.

"Tell me you fucking want this," he said, but there was no venom in his words. The monster's words were dripping with lust.

My voice was desperate. "Please. I want it."

I heard him unbuckle his belt, heard it sliding through its loops, and I tensed, waiting, only he didn't hit me. There was no torrent of thrashes or promises of how he was going to hurt me. Not this time. "Tell me you want it, Elaine. Make me believe how much you want it."

It was an amazing rush, to have to convince Lucian Morelli that I wanted him to hurt me before he would hit me. I looked back at him over my shoulder with pleading eyes. "Please, Lucian. I really do want it. I promise you I want it. I need it. I need *you*."

He trailed the leather across my ass, and I clenched. "Make me believe you want it, sweetheart," he whispered, and I felt it right down in my stomach.

He said sweetheart like he meant it, because he did. I really was his sweetheart.

Not just his doll.

My eyes must have spoken as loud as my voice when I gave him the words.

"Please, please, I want it. I want your belt on my ass. Please give me your belt on my ass. Please…" I was so ready for it when he hit me. One, *yes*. Two, *yes*. Three, *yes!*

I cried out on the fourth thrash, and he paused, waiting as I rocked, then stilled.

He waited for me to be ready for the fifth thrash. My God, he waited for me to be ready.

Lucian was a master at mastering me. His touch was incredible, teasing then thrashing, teasing then thrashing. The sensations blurred between pleasure and pain, like they normally did, only this time there was more to it. I was being guided, played like a violin by a man who wanted to play me right.

My ass was hurting almost too much to bear by the time he flipped me onto my back, arching me tightly over the sofa arm. My flesh was throbbing, raw. Divine.

"Are you going to trust me?" he asked, and his

eyes were so sincere in their beautiful power, no longer a foe.

The nod of my head was genuine. "Yes, Lucian, I'm going to trust you. I do trust you."

I did trust him. I trusted a Morelli. The very idea was insane, but it was true. I trusted Lucian Morelli more than I trusted anyone, even more than I trusted myself.

"Spread your legs nice and wide for me, Elaine," he said, and I did it without hesitation.

I stretched my thighs wide open and presented myself for him, wet and wanting. He brushed his thumb against my clit and let out a gorgeous moan.

"You are a beautiful creature. Your sweet blonde pussy is to die for." He smirked at his own words. "It is though, isn't it? Your sweet blonde pussy is literally to die for. I'll be a dead man for my crimes."

"I'll be a dead woman for wanting you back," I whispered. "We'll both be dead, Lucian."

His smile made my belly flutter along with my clit. "At least we'd die happy."

I couldn't hold back a giggle. "I'd die happier than I've ever been in my life."

His thumb was working magic on my clit, and my ass was still throbbing underneath me. I could have laid there for a lifetime enjoying it, watching him. It was him who coaxed me to more.

"Trust me, baby," he whispered and then he raised his hand. "Keep those legs spread nice and wide. I'm gonna take your pussy in so many more ways than one."

I would keep my legs spread as wide for him as I could for as long as I lived. I held them up high, offering him everything. I knew he was going to slap me where it hurt the most, and I wanted it. People had hurt me in so many ways before, but never because I wanted them to, and never with such care in their eyes.

I cried out when he slapped my pussy nice and hard, but I kept my legs spread. I bucked and cried and squirmed as he hit me over and over, but it didn't matter, I still kept my legs spread wide. He hurt my pussy, and I loved him for it.

"You're such a good girl," he told me, and it made me glow inside.

I'd always wanted to be a good girl for someone I loved.

I was a good girl as he teased my nipples then twisted my tits until I cried out for him. He did it slowly enough that I was begging for more, seeking the pain.

"Please fuck me," I asked more than once. But he didn't.

We were there for hours in the living room, and all of those hours were about me and not him. He gave me every scrap of his attention and care and time. Even when I tried to grab for his cock, he wouldn't let me. It was all about my body. He took care of me.

I was exhausted, burning and breaking in the most incredible of ways when he made me come for the third time over. I was sweating and smiling and lost in my bliss, and the monster was smiling right back at me as he grabbed my arms and pulled me up to my feet, then against him.

"You are one tired little doll," he told me, then wrapped me up tight in his arms. "How about we get Chef Morelli to make you some dinner, hmm?"

I couldn't stop my laugh as I held him back. "Yes, please."

Chapter Thirty-Two

Lucian

I'D NEVER ENJOYED doing anything for anyone. Gratitude meant nothing to me other than weakness. It was an entirely new sensation to enjoy doing things for Elaine.

I enjoyed making her come until she was a quivering mess, and hurting her in a way her body ate up in bliss, and most surprisingly of all I enjoyed making her pasta while she watched me.

She looked more beautiful than ever as she stood by my side at the kitchen counter, swamped in one of my clean shirts from the wardrobe. Her hair was wild, and her eyes were wide, and her grin was wide to match.

I knew one thing for certain before I'd even finished slicing the salami. I was going to enjoy hurting the people who'd hurt her. I was going to savor every fucking second of it.

"Have you quit the family company, then?" she asked me, with a twinkle in her eyes as I stirred the pasta. "Or is that still a big secret? Is it still none of my business?"

I couldn't hold back a smile. "I'm taking a vacation."

"A vacation?" she asked, then laughed. "I can't imagine you ever taking a vacation."

"You and the rest of the people who know me."

It was a very true observation on her part. I couldn't recall ever taking a vacation in my life. I hated non-productive time. "So...where are we going on this vacation?" she laughed. "A beach resort somewhere amazing?"

I tipped my head with a smirk. "Bishop's Landing. I've heard there is a nice little country-side house which needs some gardening work."

I loved the way she grinned.

We ate in silence as we munched at our pasta, but this time it wasn't tense; it was easy. A lovely ease between two people who really like each other's company. *Like* was an understatement, but I was still struggling with speaking the word in my own mind, even to myself. Two people who really *love* each other's company.

I couldn't remember the last time someone

had looked at me with love in their eyes like Elaine did for me. It was a stunning thing. Her eyes had never looked like such magical pools of blue as they did when they were filled with happy adoration. I'd never grow tired of looking back at them. I could only assume that mine were filled with a sheen of adoration to match. Even the thought was still too bizarre to imagine.

Still, I may be a *lover*, but I was a hater, too. The love for Elaine fueled the evil inside me in other directions, and it fueled it hard. I despised the men who'd broken her pretty little soul when she was a sweet young butterfly with innocent wings. I'd always enjoyed hurting people, but I'd never wanted it with the passion I felt down deep as I thought about tearing those sickos to pieces.

"You going to curl up with me on the sofa like a boyfriend?" Elaine teased as she collected my dish from me. "Is that what you are now? Are you my boyfriend?" She was joking. Her humor was all over her face. I didn't answer her humor with more. My reply was deadly serious.

"I've never been a boyfriend in my life. I've never even been close. This situation is entirely new ground."

"Yeah, well, I've never been a girlfriend, either." She laughed. "I was being silly, not serious.

I'm hardly going to be talking marriage and kids next, am I? Just because we like playing around with orgasms and eating pasta together doesn't mean we're suddenly soulmates."

"It would be hard to be soulmates with someone who's soulless," I told her. "Believe me, sweetheart. I'm pretty damn soulless."

Her eyes were wide as she looked at me. "Yesterday, I would've believed you."

I couldn't find a reply to that. The whole concept of having a soul and a girlfriend and any kind of romance was enough to make me feel strangely fluffy inside, and I didn't like fluffy. Fluffy was for pathetic wimps and pussies.

Even in my *fluffy* loved-up state I couldn't bring myself to curl up on the sofa with Elaine and watch shit on TV. I made for an early night, and she headed up along with me with no mention of the room down the hallway. She climbed straight on into my bed along with me once we were done with our showers.

"Are you going to actually fuck me soon?" she asked as I pulled her close under the covers.

"It's the jewel in the crown," I said. "When I take it, I'll be taking it slowly. It'll be worth waiting for."

Her little giggle was cute. "I've been waiting

quite a lot of years for it. I'm sure a little while longer isn't going to hurt."

Her sweet little yawn was divine. Even the most innocent things she did made her a pure temptress.

I wish I could have gone to sleep when she did. Her flutters of breath were sweet against my chest. I held onto her as she slept, loving the heat from her and thinking about how fucking bizarre my life was turning out to be. I hadn't given a thought to Seamus or Duncan or Morelli Holdings. I'd been thinking of nothing but Elaine since the very second I left the office that morning and came speeding back home to find her outside.

Home.

This was really home now. Elaine was my home.

Elaine was the jewel in my crown.

For the first time in my life, I felt I needed to do more to deserve it, to *earn* that particular treasure.

She was still sleeping as I eased out from beside her, settling down into the covers like an angel. I made sure I was out of her view when I finally accepted my own need for revenge against those who hurt Elaine and my need to do it now. I had been planning on starting with Colonel

Hardwick or the pricks on the charity auction scene, but no. I had one person at the forefront of my mind that night.

The first piece of shit to touch her.

I was aching with the need to destroy someone when I checked out *Reverend Lynch* online. Interestingly enough, he wasn't all that far from Bishop's Landing. He was at an abbey down at Renyard Lake, only twenty minutes down the road back toward New York City.

Hmm. Maybe there was such a thing as fate after all.

As soon as I saw the details of his manor online I felt the surge of evil in me down deep. There was no way I could fight it, not even for a single minute longer. The man had to suffer, and he had to suffer soon. Him and the others, one by one. I'd enjoy destroying every single one of them.

I checked that Elaine was still sleeping like a baby and headed on out to the car in the middle of the night. I left a scrawled note on the kitchen counter with a *Be back soon, baby*, sarcastic, like I really was going to get any good at being a *boyfriend*. The roads were empty as I sped toward Renyard Lake. My brain was churning like an evil bastard as I plotted the ways I was going to hurt him. So many options, so many of them appeal-

200

ing enough to make my pulse race.

I'd packed a blade from the kitchen in my glovebox. A gun would be far too impersonal. I wanted to get up close. Pointed and sadistic. I wanted to see the fear in his eyes as I exacted Elaine's revenge.

The manor was on top of me before I'd even registered I was there. It was a sprawling thing, slightly back from the lane. It was the easiest thing in the world to pull into the driveway. It would be the easiest thing in the world to kill him too, considering the security around this place was non-existent. Still, it would be, wouldn't it? Who would ever be heading out here to kill a reverend?

I felt sick in my gut as I waited for an answer, imagining all too clearly how Elaine's sweet little body must have been shaking when she arrived at this place every weekend. When the door swung open it was an old woman standing there. Her expression was little more than a scowl.

I remembered Elaine's secret. I remembered the nasty woman who'd led her through the house. "Margaret?" I asked, and the old woman nodded.

"Yeah…" she said, with a tip of her head. "And you are…?"

"Lucian Morelli," I told her. "Reverend Lynch

should be expecting me."

She stared at me with piercing eyes under the porch light. "At almost midnight?"

"Morelli," I reminded her.

"Hmm. Come inside then," she offered, and I did it. I stepped over that threshold with a smile on my face.

I could've taken her out along with him, breaking her neck in a heartbeat, but I didn't. I wanted to use her to scope the place out for everything it was. My eyes were fixed on our surroundings as we passed by, my head still full of everything Elaine would have been seeing and feeling when she was walking the same road. It was a disgusting façade of religion. I hated it with every fucking bone in my body. This was a new thing for me. I'd never hated anything with such vigor as I did this shithole and everything it stood for.

"Wait here, please," she told me, and stepped away along the hall once we'd turned a corner.

I was expecting it when she came gliding back out of there with a puzzled expression on her face.

"The reverend says he doesn't know what you're talking about," she told me. "He has no recollection of any appointment with you."

"It will be a shame if I came all this way for

nothing. I suppose my assistant didn't make the arrangements correctly. It wouldn't be the first time. Good help is hard to find."

She was the one to buckle. "I guess you should head in and speak to him yourself. He's right up the hallway to the right."

"Thank you," I told her. "I'll most certainly speak to him myself."

She didn't hang around to watch me make my move. She was off in a flash as there was a clatter from the floor upstairs. I wondered just who was up there and whether he still had a whole host of pure, sweet girls being used for his fun.

I guessed I'd be finding out soon enough.

The knife was already in my hand by the time I knocked on the door.

"Enter!"

I stepped over that threshold with a grim smile.

Chapter Thirty-Three

Elaine

H E WAS GONE when I woke up in the middle of the night. A terrified part of me thought that he'd come to his senses somehow and walked out of my hopes and dreams. That's what I was having—hopes and dreams that I hadn't had since I was a little girl.

I may have joked about marriage and kids with my *boyfriend,* Lucian, but it wasn't such a joke inside. I did want it all with the monster. The monster was everything I wanted and more.

I called out Lucian's name before I switched on the bedside light and looked around me. He was definitely gone. I slipped out of bed and checked the bathroom but nothing. He wasn't downstairs in the living room, and the kitchen was empty to match. I was reaching for a glass for some mineral water when I saw the note on the counter—scribbled, just like the one I'd left on mine. Only Lucian's scribbled note was hilarious. It lit me up inside.

Be back soon, baby.

I could imagine the smirk on his face as he wrote it. I was getting to know his expressions so damn well. Smirk, frown, scowl—and sometimes, like a ray of sun through his dark demeanor, a smile. Only for me.

Going back to bed was an appealing option, but I couldn't do it. My brain wouldn't have switched off enough to let me sleep. I flinched as I dropped onto the sofa and curled my legs up tight. I was still hurting, my flesh sore from the monster's touch. It was magical in the very best of ways. He'd made it feel as good for me as it could possibly feel.

The TV was full of crap that didn't interest me. My mind was full of Lucian. Lucian and me, Lucian and life, Lucian and our future.

How the hell could we have a future?

We'd never be allowed to have a future. If anyone ever saw us together, they'd kill us for our betrayal.

I'd never really thought about just what was so unforgivable between the Morellis and the Constantines. I knew we'd hated each other since long before I was born, but the logic had never really been explained to me. I guess I'd asked when I was still young enough to ask such questions, but likely got the same universal response.

The Morellis are worthy of nothing. They are our enemy. They've been out to destroy us for all time.

I knew they had made every effort to undermine us in New York City life, and business, and deals. There was more to it, too. So many people believed it had been a Morelli who had killed my father. There was no doubt about it to any of my family—it must have been one of the Morellis. They'd been assholes at every opportunity—despising us as much as we despised them, enough to murder the man at the very top of the family tree—but why? I wasn't sure I really knew why. It would have been so bad if the hate was based on the very first thing I'd ever heard of between us—one original act that caused a divide between two men and the one woman they wanted. My mother. But it *was* that...of course it was...both men had fallen for my mother to the point they'd destroyed everything else for the chance of having her. Two men, one prize, and no damn way of sharing it.

My father had won. Caroline Roosevelt had become Caroline Constantine, and Bryant Morelli had been unable to accept my father's victory.

The battle must have been a rough one.

They hated each other from the moment my father took his bride. Now *we* hated each other. Every single one of us hated each other.

Or we used to. Before me and Lucian fell in love and broke tradition.

I let the thoughts simmer for long minutes, thinking it through, over and over. I hated the Morellis, right? They were assholes worth hating. For sure they were. Every single one of them was a piece of shit—apart from Lucian—and all that stuff between our families must have been a long time brewing with a whole load of backbone to it. Bryant Morelli and my father were close friends growing up. Surely it couldn't have only been my mother that tore them apart.

Lucian *must* know some stuff. There must be a whole stack of stuff that led to the war between two families who used to like each other.

I was kidding myself. Of course I was. I knew full well, in instinct as much as in sense, that it was my mother who destroyed them—just like she tore everything apart. She'd caused us a family divide destined to end in death for so many names on the family trees.

Maybe mine and Lucian's deaths would be next.

The thought made me shiver, and that made me smile just a little to myself. Oh, how quickly things can change. There was no doubt about it. Not in the slightest. I didn't want to die anymore. I wanted to live forever, for all time, for every breath I could possibly breathe in this world.

In *his* world.

I wanted it all alongside Lucian Morelli.

Chapter Thirty-Four

Lucian

H E WAS A pathetic looking man. Even more pathetic than I'd imagined. His pitiful face was shallow and vile. His eyes were beady and his lips were pursed. Hardly a welcoming reverend by anyone's standards. I'm sure my eyes were as evil as they'd ever been as I closed the distance between us.

"Lucian Morelli?" he asked, and his voice was weakly curious. "I wasn't expecting you. Do you wish to be a member of the fellowship?"

I stepped up to one of the pictures on his wall. It was a garish piece of crap showing a benevolent Lord Jesus reaching down toward the children at his feet. "Tell me about this *fellowship*," I said, feigning interest. "I heard you used to offer Elaine Constantine as a benefit of membership."

His smile made me rage like a beast inside.

"Ah yes, Elaine," he said, and his expression was one of relief. "Unfortunately, Elaine is now grown up. She was a delightful creature, but she outgrew us as they all do. We have other girls who are very similar though."

I didn't speak to him, just stared until he continued talking. "I really didn't believe the Morellis wanted to be a part of this fellowship. I didn't believe you crossed over with the Constantines. Lionel was adamant that you didn't." He paused. "May I ask who introduced you to our order?"

"One of the Constantines," I told him, and he let out a laugh.

"That's quite a surprise. I really didn't expect there to be any communication between you and the Constantines. I guess our world is changing. We can thank the Lord for his blessing in friendship."

"We can certainly thank the Lord for my presence here," I said.

"Take a seat," he offered and gestured to the chair opposite him. "We can discuss the options. Joining the order is expensive, but most certainly worth the investment. Our handshake goes a very long way in this world."

I took the seat, leaning back and crossing my

legs at the knee like a truly relaxed potential member. My gloved hands flexed, fingers stretching.

"Who else does this handshake belong to? I want to know exactly who I'm signing up with."

He paused. "I'm not permitted to disclose the full details of the order until after initiation into our group. I can assure you that our members are very established fellows who would be extremely pleased to have a man of your stature among them. I must say I'm pleasantly surprised by your interest."

I didn't speak, just sat there. I had two options available to me. I either tortured him until he gave me the member list slowly, or I got the piece of shit to spill all before I knifed him. Or both. I opted for both.

"I want the membership list, or I'm out of here. I'm not joining with nobodies or pussies."

The standoff lasted seconds, not minutes.

His shrug was as pathetic as he was. "If it was one of the Constantines that told you about us, I'm certain you're outside of the usual precautions. We have no nobodies or pussies in our order, I can assure you. We are limited in our numbers. Quite exclusive," he simpered.

"I know of Rawlings, Eddington, and Hardwick," I told him. "I've heard they are particularly brutal beasts with the girls."

He smirked at me. "Oh yes. They are brutal with the girls. They very much enjoyed Elaine, you know." His eyes fogged over with memory. "She took her punishment like a good girl."

I could have ripped his balls off and rammed them down his throat there and then. "Who else enjoys playtime?" I asked him. "Tell me."

The Reverend betrayed his members so casually. "Lionel. Anthony Ellison. Carlos Madeira. Cederic Bartonshire," he informed me. "A lot of our members are from across the Atlantic, of course. Their aristocratic scene over there is very...seeking. As I said though, it's quite exclusive. That's the full list."

I could imagine it. Already my mind was running away, picturing routes overseas and just what the fuck I was going to do with them.

"Do enlighten me," Lynch said. "Who told you about us? Surely it was Lionel, yes?"

That's when I picked my moment. "It was Elaine."

"Elaine Constantine?" he asked, and his shock was delicious.

"Yes," I told him. "It was Elaine."

He realized I wasn't the potential member I'd

presented myself as.

He moved as quickly as I did, but I was faster than that incompetent piece of shit. He darted for his exit, but I darted for him, tumbling him back onto his seat before he was even out of it. He crashed onto his back, staring up at me with panicked piggy eyes.

My foot was on his chest in an instant, pressing hard. He didn't even try to push me off.

"Why are you doing this?" he asked me. "For her? For that little girl who lied as well as she took cock? She's nothing!"

"She's everything, but most importantly—" I leaned over and spat in his face. "She's *mine.*"

"But she's a-a Constantine." His confusion was obvious. Mine would have been obvious to match his just a few days ago.

Voicing it aloud was a whole other league to me. It was a combination of disgusting and fantastic as I spoke the words. "I'm in love with Elaine Constantine."

His jaw dropped open, and his eyes were huge white plates as I pulled out the blade from my inside pocket. "This is some ploy to get close to the Constantines, isn't it? Let me up from here and I will tell you all you need to know about them. I'll tell you all about Elaine. We didn't mean to hurt her. She enjoyed it. She enjoyed being a fellowship girl."

He was hoping for a miracle.

"I know everything I need to know about her Constantine background," I told him. "I know everything I need to know about *you.*"

I pressed my foot to his throat. His hands gripped my ankle as he squirmed, but I wouldn't budge, just kept my weight at a beautiful enough pressure to make him choke and turn red. Wriggling piece of shit.

"I'm going to enjoy this," I said, and lowered the blade.

I stripped that man with my knife before I hurt him. I kicked him in the face as he tried to scream, busting his jaw so bad he was a mess, and then I took it slowly. Each slice of my blade was a thrill to me, only this time it wasn't about my addiction to inflicting pain. This time it was all about the woman I was avenging.

It was about her beautiful eyes and how they must have cried when this man touched her. It was about him punishing her over so much time that she believed she deserved it.

It was about the way he'd touched her, the way he'd whispered filth into her ear when she was too broken to understand what he was doing to her.

It was about the way he'd been in this place, letting other men in for their sick thrills at her expense—my beautiful girl with a heart of gold.

I did things to the sick fuck that made even my stomach turn. He was a gurgling wreck as I finally took the ultimate payback.

I leaned in close, whispering right into his wheezing face.

"This is for Elaine," I said. "Say hello to the Lord and Savior when you get there. I'm sure he'll be pleased to see you, you disgusting piece of shit." I pushed the blade straight through his windpipe and twisted it.

I had a smile on my face as he gurgled his final breath. I was covered in blood as I left his body on the floor and smoothed my bloodstained jacket down over my chest.

Chapter Thirty-Five

Elaine

LUCIAN'S CAR PULLED up as dawn was just beginning to creep in. The low rumble of the engine woke me from my daze on the sofa, the headlights bright enough in the dark to shine through the window. He was home. My *boyfriend* was home.

That word felt strange. It didn't describe the wild, twisted, mad way that I loved Lucian, but I also cherished it. Such a simple, carefree declaration: *my boyfriend.*

Just thinking it made my heart leap.

I was already on my feet and at the front door when he stepped up to the porch. I was all set to dash out and grab him, but I stopped as he came into view under the porch light.

My *boyfriend* was covered in blood, and it most certainly wasn't his own. His shirt was splattered, red on white. His jacket was damp and his face was smeared with red to match. His gloved fingers were bloodied around his keys, and his eyes were shining dark.

Evil. But it wasn't evil directed at me…

I didn't even know what questions to ask. They were empty sounds in my mouth. I stepped back to let him through, and he walked in with purpose and strength, as powerful as I'd ever seen him. Then he smiled. Lucian Morelli, covered in blood, smiled at me.

"Morning, sweetheart."

He headed straight to the kitchen, flicking on the coffee machine before ditching his gloves in the sink. He got out two mugs and went to work, mute, without offering a single word.

It was me who finally found my voice and asked the most obvious question.

"What happened?"

His eyes were twinkling when they met mine. "I had some business."

"Business?"

He laughed. "Yes, sweetheart, business. Business for *you*."

I looked him up and down, still trying to soak in what the hell was happening. "For *me?* How the hell could this be for *me?*"

He leaned against the counter casually, like this wasn't some kind of alternate dimension of craziness at dawn. "Well, that depends on who the blood belonged to, doesn't it?"

I got a shiver all the way through me, because it couldn't be…it couldn't be from someone who hurt me. But it was. Of course it was. My stomach did the weirdest lurch. My heart was racing at the thought—both excited and scared at once.

"Who was it?" I asked, then took a breath. "Was it Uncle Lionel?"

Even the thought was terrifying—because if it was Uncle Lionel and people knew—if people knew, they would put the pieces together and those pieces would spell MORELLI in huge capital letters, and MORELLI would spell out LUCIAN Morelli the very moment it was said out loud.

Only it wasn't Uncle Lionel.

"It was Reverend fucking Lynch," he told me. "I tore the piece of shit apart."

I stared in shock. Lucian had killed the man who'd prepared me for punishment and made me take it at the hands of other men. My mortal enemy of just a few days ago had ripped apart the man who'd been my true enemy since I was a little girl.

"You killed Reverend Lynch?" I asked him.

He gave me a smirk. "I most certainly killed him, Elaine. I'm sure he was damn well pleased when I did. He was hardly enjoying his last few moments alive, I can promise you that."

The thought of Reverend Lynch suffering was strangely nice. Even buried after all these years, it was nice to think of him hurting, just like all the times he'd enjoyed my pain. Only he was *dead*. Lucian had killed him. Reverend Lynch was actually dead.

It shouldn't have surprised me, because this was Lucian Morelli standing before me, and Lucian Morelli was undoubtedly the most vicious man alive. He hurt people for fun and fascination. He arranged deaths for his own ends, whenever it suited him. What surprised me was that his own hands were dirty, and it was because of me. He'd killed someone for me. Again. He'd killed someone because they'd hurt *me*.

I'm not sure it was everyone's traditional idea of *boyfriend material* but in a fucked-up little part of my soul it sure felt like it to me.

My next words were a whisper as I tried to digest it. "Reverend Lynch is dead."

Lucian poured my coffee. "I also made sure the girls' doors were open before I left the place, even though they were sleeping soundly."

"Wow." He'd killed them and freed the girls.
I smiled at him. Those girls would have been
going through so much, just like I was. The
monster had freed the victims.

"Thanks," I said, and it was the most pathetic
word in the world.

"You're very welcome, Elaine." His eyes were
fire on mine. "He will be the first of many."

"Many?"

His grin made me light up inside. "Many.
Believe me, baby, I have a whole list of the next
candidates. I'll be savoring every single one of
them."

My brain was spinning just thinking about it.
I was still trying to comprehend whether I was
reading this right, because if I was... "You mean
people alongside Reverend Lynch?"

"I mean every man who has ever laid his sick
twisted hands on your sweet little body. Payback
will be divine," he said.

Yeah, he was certainly *boyfriend material*. I
didn't know what to do so I did nothing, still
trying to get a grip on my thoughts. I took my
mug from him with shaking fingers, still blown
away by just how casual the monster was in the
aftermath of butchering someone up close.

I stared at him, loving him. The full weight of what he'd done for me slammed me like a train when I finally came to my senses enough to process it. Reverend Lynch was dead, and the girls around him were free. I'm not sure who was more surprised when I launched myself at Lucian's body and wrapped my arms around his neck. He was still wet with blood, but I didn't care. All I cared about was being up close to the man I loved.

I didn't just love Lucian Morelli, I adored him. I adored him as much as it could ever be possible to adore someone. He was like a god to me—a beautiful, vicious god who'd killed for me like a noble avenger.

"Thank you," I whispered, and this time it came out from deep in my heart. "Thank you for loving me, Lucian."

He pushed me away just far enough to look me in the eyes.

"I told him I loved you, you know," he growled. "I told that bastard I was in love with you before I knifed him to death."

The thought made me proud. It filled me with glee that Reverend Lynch knew that finally someone loved me enough to make him pay for his sins. Just a shame it was one of the Morellis and not the Constantines.

Lucian ran his thumb down my cheek, then pressed his lips to mine. His kiss tasted like blood, but I didn't care. I'd already kissed him in someone else's blood. Both times were because he was hurting them for hurting me. Boyfriend material didn't even come close to it on reflection.

"What did you do with the body?" I asked. "Is it just lying there? The police will come find it, right? Will they know it was you?"

His laugh was depraved. "Lynch's body is in the trunk outside," he said.

"In the trunk?" The whole thing was growing more bizarre by the second.

"In the trunk. They'll find plenty of blood in that fuck-up of a manor, but they won't find him. The police might well find the scene, but they won't be coming after me. The *fellowship* will be damned sure his death stays well hidden."

"Oh, thank god." The relief when I heard that was a beautiful thing. The idea of Lucian being arrested and taken away from me was becoming the most unbearable thing in the world.

"And that Margaret will be out of the country by the time the cops find anything. I told her to run if she wanted to live."

I held him tight again, breathing against him,

grateful to have him in my arms. I wanted nothing but Lucian for all time. I wanted him at my side through every step I took, right to the end of my life. I couldn't be away from him if I tried. I'd never make it. I'd never want to make it.

"I mean it," he whispered. "I'll kill them all, baby, one by one. They'll all rue the day they ever looked at you that way, let alone touched you. That's a promise."

His warmth against me was blissful, even soaked in blood. I squeezed him, kissed him, did everything I could to let him know just how much I loved him, and then I asked him all over again.

"Please, Lucian, please will you fuck me now? I need to feel you inside me, please."

He brushed my hair from my forehead and smiled down at me with dark, sparkling eyes. "Yes, sweetheart, I'll fuck you now. It's time."

CHAPTER THIRTY-SIX

Lucian

ELAINE CONSTANTINE'S SWEET virgin pussy was the greatest jewel in the crown there could possibly be. It was still amazing to me that taking the prize mattered less to me than how much she would enjoy me taking it. But still, I wanted her to gasp and beg, desperate for every second.

She wanted kisses. She wanted holding. She wanted *me*.

I was drenched through to the skin with the reverend's blood. I dropped my jacket onto the kitchen floor and it landed with a damp thump on the tile. Elaine's fingers were already on my shirt buttons as I guided her through to the living room. Fingers that were shaking, just like the rest of her, only it wasn't fear that was making her quake for me this time. It was a whole other type of nervousness; I could see it in her beautiful eyes. Those pools of crystal blue were light and delicate, even in the dull of the pre-dawn. They were eating me up with a devotion I'd never seen before. I'd never *felt* before.

It was a beautiful thing to witness, just how surprised and moved she was by someone caring about her. There should have been a whole army of men in her life tearing down walls to destroy anyone who dared to fuck her over in the slightest, but that army had never existed. Her family was fake, each and every one of the sad fuckers too far up their own self-important assholes, casting her aside for telling lies when all she wanted was for someone to hear her truth.

I'd heard her truth. I'd avenged her truth with the very first vile bastard who deserved it.

I was already aching to get started on the next one on the list.

Elaine was still kissing me as we reached the bottom of the staircase. I tore the bloodied shirt from my shoulders, and she was already at my belt, unbuckling as we climbed the stairs.

I never thought I'd be desperate to take a virgin in my bed. I usually wanted them on all fours, begging for their first cock, or making them force themselves down onto my cock, not enjoying the comfort of the mattress like a princess with her legs spread beautifully wide for me.

"You're really going to do it?" she said as we reached the top of the stairs. "You're really going to take me?"

The nip of my teeth on her throat said more than words. The way I shunted her toward my bedroom screamed volumes.

I dropped my pants and kicked them aside before we reached the doorway. My hands were on the oversized shirt on Elaine's body, tearing it from her tiny frame.

She thought I was going to throw her down onto the bed and take my fill of her, I could see it by the way she backed up against the bed ready for me. I didn't. As usual, I surprised her.

I tugged her into the bathroom, still squeezing tight as I flicked on the shower. It was steaming in no time, the water pumping hard and fast in the little shell of a cubicle. I opened the screen nice and wide and guided Elaine in first, pressing her up against the back wall as I stepped in alongside her.

Steaming didn't even come close as I claimed her mouth as mine. I consumed her, tongue to tongue. I ate her up like a starving man, and she ate me up right back as I grabbed up the soap and lathered her body.

She was my girl, and I was going to treat her like one. Maybe *boyfriend* wasn't so far off the mark after all.

Maybe I, Lucian Morelli, really was Elaine Constantine's *boyfriend*. It gave me another one of those damn fluffy tingles to think of being a damn sight more than that, too.

Maybe I, Lucian Morelli, wanted Elaine Constantine to be my damn bride.

"I'm so nervous," she told me over the hiss of the water. "I've been waiting for this for years, and I never thought it would really mean anything, but now I'm here, ready. Now that it's with you, it means so much."

I wanted to kiss every inch of her until she was ready for everything that was coming. In the haze of how much I wanted the girl in front of me, I lost all sense of time, of urgency, of *me*.

I thumbed her clit just enough to make her grind against my hand before I slipped two fingers inside her and curled them. She supported her weight on my shoulders, moaning as she rocked, and I twisted my fingers inside her, just enough to make her whimper. She was tight, so fucking tight. Taking her sweet little pussy would definitely still hurt her. The thought made my mouth water and my cock swell.

I worked her soft skin slowly under the pummeling water. Kissing, stroking, squeezing. My fingers played her until the morning was bright outside the bathroom window, teasing her softly enough that when she came for me she was a bucking mess against my hand.

I guess it was when her sweet breaths were shallow on my face through the steam that the beast in me reared its head through the fluffy bullshit. I loved Elaine Constantine with every scrap of my fucked-up soul, but that didn't stop what I needed. What my *cock* needed. What my filthy fucking mind needed.

I flicked off the shower and reached for the towels from the rail. She must have seen my expression change because her eyes widened big and blue as she stared up at me.

I saw it in her gaze. There she was again, my opposite. The masochist to my sadist. The pain toy inside her was ready to dance with the beast.

Elaine wanted me to be rough with her. She wanted to be my little doll.

"Don't make it nice," she whispered, before I'd said a word. "Please, Lucian. I want to know what you're like. I want to feel you as you."

I felt my smirk and recognized myself as the true Morelli I'd always been.

"Don't worry, sweetheart, you'll feel me as me," I told her. "It's gonna be one hell of a fucking ride."

Chapter Thirty-Seven

Elaine

I WAS ALREADY learning so much about the dynamic between me and Lucian. We shifted so much from minute to minute, so naturally I didn't even feel the twist. Kind, then cruel, in the kindest of ways. The monster found his claws as he threw me onto the bed. I was still wet from the shower and so was he, both of us hot and steaming, and that just made it all the more beautiful as he slammed his body down onto mine.

His kiss was tongue and teeth, pain and pleasure. His breaths were heavy and hot, and his hands were savage as they sought out my tits and twisted my flesh until I moaned for him.

This was what I wanted.

I wanted the monster to claim me as his, lust and love dancing together in a blur. I wanted to be owned by Lucian Morelli and I wanted to feel him possess me, his body taking mine with every breath.

My skin was tingling, on fire in the flames. I knew this was it. The beast was really going to take me.

My legs spread so naturally for him, wrapping up and around his waist. My clit was still thrumming, alive from his attention in the shower.

He didn't let my legs hold him for long. He pulled them apart and licked a path down my body. He bit my nipples and pulled them sharp. I whimpered. He bit them harder.

His teeth were bliss as they nipped their way down my stomach. My hips were already rising from the bed to meet his mouth as his tongue found my clit all over again.

"Please!" I whimpered. "Please, Lucian, just take me! Take me!"

His eyes were dark with lust. "Quiet."

One word, but it put me in my place. Lucian was the monster, just like always. He was *my* monster. My *true* monster.

I forced myself to relax into the bed, biting my lip as he worked his fingers inside me, slowly enough to make me buck for more. He slapped my thighs when I moved against him.

"Be still!" he ordered, and I loved it—that viciousness in his beautiful voice.

I was still for him. I took his fingers like a good girl, unable to hold back the moans as he sucked gently at my clit.

I wasn't expecting it when he took his fingers from my pussy and twisted them into my ass. I cried out but took everything he had to give me, smiling at the ceiling as he circled his fingers deeper, opening me up. *YES!* His tongue lapped at my ass and I wanted more. I wanted him as deep inside me as he could go, in every hole, not just my pussy. *Everywhere.* I wanted him every-where. I wanted him to own every part of me and show me I was his toy as well as his love.

"Yes! Fuck me there," I breathed. "Please. Fuck my ass."

"Your ass can wait its turn." He slapped my thighs. He slapped my pussy. He fingered my ass until I squirmed and begged for more.

He gave me whatever he wanted, and nothing more.

My body was so tense with sensations that I'd lost control of what the hell I was feeling by the time the monster climbed back up on top of me. His lips were puffy from where he'd been playing with me. They were hot and wet when they met with mine, and his tongue tasted of me.

His cock was swollen hard and thick when he ground it against my clit, the rhythm of his hips so natural against mine that we were one together. This time he didn't pull my legs away when they wrapped around his waist and gripped tight. I could barely believe it after all this time. My virginity was about to leave me behind.

"Time for me to take the crown jewel," he whispered, and he took it.

Lucian Morelli thrust his cock inside me in one slam of his hips and claimed me as his.

It stole my breath and hurt like hell, but I loved the way it felt. The way he felt deep inside me was every bit as magical as I'd dreamed it would be.

His hips were slow but powerful. His smile was both loving and dark at the same time.

He pinned my wrists above my head and crushed them tight to the bed, holding me in position as he picked up the pace and fucked me harder and harder. My pussy took him, aching for more, desperate for more, even though it was hurting. I was wet but sore in the most amazing of ways, and I realized in that one incredible moment that every day I'd resented being a virgin was worth it. I would've waited a whole other decade to feel the magic I felt with the Morelli monster deep inside me. It would be worth every single minute.

"Your pussy is going to get used to this," he told me, and I smiled.

"I hope my pussy gets used to this every damn day," I said, and he smiled right back.

"Don't you worry about that, baby. I'll be claiming this beauty as mine every fucking day we're breathing." His words were enough to give me the hint of a shiver.

Every day we're breathing.

There was a body of a reverend in the trunk of his car, and two families who'd kill us just for speaking. I was a kidnap victim all over the news, and Lucian was on a *vacation* that didn't exist.

Every day we were breathing might not be all that many.

"Come inside me," I whispered. "Please. Please, come inside me."

"Want to have my baby now do you, baby girl?" His smirk was perfection. "Our story gets more and more fucking crazy, doesn't it?"

I didn't say no, because I couldn't. I couldn't laugh the crazy off as crazy. I *did* want Lucian's baby inside me. I wanted to be his bride and his love and the mother of his child. Fucked-up, but true. The whole thing was fucked-up but true. I was plunging into the pit of insanity deeper and deeper every damn minute.

"Tell me, Elaine," he rasped, right in my ear. "Say you want my baby inside you."

I felt so raw when I found the words. I'd never felt so exposed as I did when I told the beautiful monster what I wanted. "Yes, Lucian. I want your baby inside me. One day, I want *our* baby inside me."

"Good girl," he said, and then he kissed me with a smile on his face.

He was still kissing me as his hips slammed with a whole new force and his breaths grew frantic. He tipped my hips back on the bed and plowed me deeper with every thrust, and there it was, the spot that felt just right…the spot that had me floating from the bed. The spot that had my clit singing all over again. I was coming and moaning against his open mouth as he emptied his balls inside me.

Lucian Morelli came inside me. He spilled his amazing, filthy seed inside me. It was the most incredible feeling.

He didn't pull out of me when he stopped thrusting. We were both panting as he let go of my wrists and collapsed his weight on top of me. Our limbs were tangled as he turned onto his side and pulled me with him, wrapping me tight in his arms.

I was grinning as my pussy throbbed, sore but loving it. I wasn't a virgin anymore. Whoa. The very thought had me grinning.

"The king takes his crown jewel," he said and tipped my face up to his. "It was every bit worth waiting for, Miss Constantine."

I giggled, high on life and not coke. It was an amazing contrast. "I hope the king can take the crown jewel again real soon," I told him, and he laughed along with me.

His cock was already hard against my belly as he flipped me onto my back. "Don't worry about that, sweetheart," he said. "And this time I'm gonna make it hurt."

He wasn't lying.

He made it hurt.

Bites and bruises and blood. Force and fight and filth.

And love.

So much love it chased my demons away.

CHAPTER THIRTY-EIGHT

Lucian

I STARED DOWN at the freshly shoveled flower bed with a smile on my face, my arm wrapped around the woman I loved in a way I didn't believe was possible for this twisted heart of mine to love.

Elaine had been a darling with the spade, helping me in my mission to dig the grave with a sweet little smile on her face.

She didn't speak and neither did I. Words weren't needed.

Already the world churned around us. So many questions with our names all over them. Disappearance. Kidnapping. Morellis and Constantines.

I didn't care about any of it. Not anymore.

All I cared about was my devotion to the woman at my side, and just how the fucking hell we were going to forge a way for ourselves.

This property on Bishop's Landing wasn't going to be enough of a *home* to keep us together. People would be coming, seeking, demanding. They hadn't looked for her here yet, but they would figure it out soon enough. Even my connections and my power wouldn't keep the authorities out, if they knew I had Elaine held hostage.

People would be wanting to kill us the very moment they caught sight of the truth.

I kissed Elaine's head and held her tighter.

There was no doubt about it, we'd committed the most forbidden crime we could have committed, and it wasn't the reverend's body at our feet.

A Morelli had fallen in love with a Constantine.

And a Constantine had fallen in love with him right back.

Our road ahead was impossible, but we'd find it. We *had* to find it.

Elaine was thinking the same thoughts as me in that beautiful head of hers. She looked up at me with a delicate smile. "What do we do now?" she asked me.

"Well, sweetheart, we can't stay here forever."

She laughed. "Life would have been a whole

lot easier if you could just keep hating me, wouldn't it? If I could have just kept hating you."

I tossed the spade to the ground. "I could never really hate you. You're too damn intoxicating for that, Elaine."

"You're pretty damn intoxicating yourself, Lucian," she said. "Cocaine has nothing on you."

I took her hand and led her back to the porch. The sky was already darkening, the afternoon reaching its close.

In truth I had no idea where the road ahead was leading us, I just knew it would be together.

"Time for the king to take my crown jewel again?" she asked me, tugging me inside with a mischievous smile on her perfect lips.

Yes, it was time for the king to take her sweet crown jewel again. The king would never grow tired of taking that pretty gem; I knew it right down in my dark, dirty soul.

They'd be coming after me, and I knew it.

Time was ticking, and it was ticking fast, but not fast enough to take away the moment.

With the smell of fresh dirt in the air, and no one else around for miles, it felt like we were alone in the world. Or like we were in some far-off place where we were untouchable.

That was an illusion, though.

We were in the heart of Bishop's Landing.

We couldn't see any of the other massive estates from here, but we knew they existed.

And we heard the vehicle before we saw it.

The gentle hum of an engine, the sound of tires on the road.

Our eyes met. The irony is that I was caught. If Elaine had wanted to be free, all she had to do was wait until she was seen. The world was looking for her. Whoever was coming would be her ticket out of my clutches.

I saw that awareness run through her mind.

I saw when she made her decision.

Maybe it was because of the body that's now six feet under. Maybe it was something else. Either way, she dashed to the house, hiding herself from view before the Bentley crested the rise.

The irony of the situation doesn't escape me. I'm standing here with a shovel and a flower bed as if I enjoy gardening. Me, Lucian Morelli. They'll think I've gone insane.

They're probably right.

I recognize this particular car.

Connor Ohanian was a man of strong loyalty. It has been very hard to get him onto my side for the takeover because he had worked with my father for so long.

He and I also worked together, of course. For years.

We worked together closely, and he trusted me. But it was only my father's risky behavior and the impact that it was having on thousands of employees that made Ohanian agree to the coup.

I hadn't spoken to him since I went on a leave of absence.

His car glides over the long driveway and pulls a few feet away. He gets out, looking the same as he always does, wearing a suit and slightly worried expression.

It's his default state. I'm not sure I've ever seen him any other way.

"Lucian," he says. "I'm sorry. I'm sorry the plan didn't work."

It's strange, but I find myself chuckling. "You know what? I've barely thought about it. Maybe everything worked out for the best."

"It didn't," he says. "Morelli Holdings is going under. Your father has become even more erratic. He's taking bigger risks. The entire company will fold if we don't do something."

It did bother me. The family, my mother, my sisters, all those employees. I cared about Morelli Holdings, but I loved Elaine more. "Not my problem. The board didn't vote me in."

"That's the thing. They're going to vote you in. It's already been decided in an emergency meeting. You're the new CEO if you're willing to take the position." He seems to notice the dirt on my hands and the freshly plowed earth. "Come with me. The vote can happen right now."

Surprise holds me still. "You're serious."

"Dead serious. Once we looked at the deals he's been signing and the numbers, we had to act. We're already facing serious layoffs, and perhaps worse. We need you."

They need me. I should be crowing at the triumph. This is exactly what I wanted to have happen. It means power. Money. It means winning over my father. I could leave Elaine in the house, attend the vote, and come back as the CEO of Morelli Holdings.

Except it's not just about the vote. It's about everything that comes after.

Early mornings and long nights of work. Righting what my father wronged. More power struggles. I couldn't go into the office every day, leaving her alone.

My little doll needed me. And maybe more than that, I needed her.

Strange that after working so hard to take over

the company, that I was now faced with a choice. Only, it wasn't really a choice, was it? I already loved Elaine. We couldn't be together in public. That would put her safety at risk. But we could be together in private.

And for now, that was enough.

✧   ✧   ✧

Thank you for reading SOULLESS! We hope you loved Lucian Morelli and Elaine Constantine's dark love story. Find out what happens next in **RELENTLESS**.

I'm an heiress with a broken past. It should have been the end for me, but now my mortal enemy has become my savior. He hides me away from the world as if he can save me.

Lucian Morelli is a billionaire who doesn't know how to feel anything.

Except when he's with me.

Love between a Morelli and a Constantine will never survive. The war between both families turns into an inferno, consuming the entire city of Bishop's Landing. The world is soaked in blood. No one is left standing, not even the couple who vowed their final breaths.

And you can read Lucian's brother Leo's love story right now!

Leo Morelli is known as the Beast of Bishop's Landing for his cruelty. He'll get revenge on the Constantine family and make millions of dollars in the process. Even it means using an old man who dreams up wild inventions.

The warring Morelli and Constantine families have enough bad blood to fill an ocean, and their brand new stories will be told by your favorite dangerous romance authors. See what books are available now and sign up to get notified about new releases here…
www.dangerouspress.com

ABOUT MIDNIGHT DYNASTY

The warring Morelli and Constantine families have enough bad blood to fill an ocean, and their brand new stories will be told by your favorite dangerous romance authors.

Meet Winston Constantine, the head of the Constantine family. He's used to people bowing to his will. Money can buy anything. And anyone. Including Ash Elliot, his new maid.

But love can have deadly consequences when it comes from a Constantine. At the stroke of midnight, that choice may be lost for both of them.

> "Brilliant storytelling packed with a powerful emotional punch, it's been years since I've been so invested in a book. Erotic romance at its finest!"
>
> – #1 New York Times bestselling author
> Rachel Van Dyken

"Stroke of Midnight is by far the hottest book I've read in a very long time! Winston Constantine is a dirty talking alpha who makes no apologies for going after what he wants."

– USA Today bestselling author
Jenika Snow

Ready for more bad boys, more drama, and more heat? The Constantines have a resident fixer. The man they call when they need someone persuaded in a violent fashion. Ronan was danger and beauty, murder and mercy.

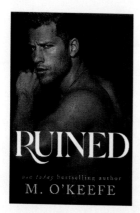

Outside a glittering party, I saw a man in the dark. I didn't know then that he was an assassin. A hit man. A mercenary. Ronan radiated danger and beauty. Mercy and mystery.

I wanted him, but I was already promised to another man. Ronan might be the one who murdered him. But two warring families want my blood. I don't know where to turn.

In a mad world of luxury and secrets, he's the only one I can trust.

"M. O'Keefe brings her A-game in this sexy, complicated romance where you're left questioning if everything you thought was true while dying to get your hands on the next book!"

– New York Times bestselling author
K. Bromberg

"Powerful, sexy, and written like a dream, RUINED is the kind of book you wish you could read forever and ever. Ronan Byrne is my new romance addiction, and I'm already pining for more blue eyes and dirty deeds in the dark."

– USA Today Bestselling Author
Sierra Simone

SIGN UP FOR THE NEWSLETTER
www.dangerouspress.com

JOIN THE FACEBOOK GROUP HERE
www.dangerouspress.com/facebook

FOLLOW US ON INSTAGRAM
www.instagram.com/dangerouspress

ABOUT THE AUTHOR

Jade has increasingly little to say about herself as time goes on, other than the fact she is an author, but she's plenty happy with this. Living in imaginary realities and having a legitimate excuse for it is really all she's ever wanted.

Jade is as dirty as you'd expect from her novels, and talking smut makes her smile.

She lives in the Herefordshire countryside with a couple of hounds and a guy who's able to cope with her inherent weirdness.

She has a red living room, decorated with far more zebra print than most people could bear, and fights a constant battle with her addiction to Coca-Cola.

Find Jade (or stalk her – she loves it) at:
facebook.com/jadewestauthor
twitter.com/jadewestauthor
jadewestauthor.com

Sign up to her newsletter, she won't spam you and you may win some goodies.
www.subscribepage.com/jadewest

COPYRIGHT

This is a work of fiction. Any resemblance to actual persons, living or dead, business establishments, events or locales is entirely coincidental. All rights reserved. Except for use in a review, the reproduction or use of this work in any part is forbidden without the express written permission of the author.

Made in United States
North Haven, CT
26 March 2022

17526677R10152